Advance Praise for *Jeremy* _____
an Aspiring Novelist

"With 120 brilliantly chisel_____
offers a mock portrait of th_ _____ _. _..ust, lampooning the
naïve literary ambitions too many of us may have suffered
through. (Several episodes hit close to home for me!) Bitingly
satirical about writing programs and professors and the
publishing world and more, also reveals a warmer, more
generous humor too—a delightfully poignant mix, with
surprises at several turns." - Art Taylor, author of *The Boy
Detective & The Summer of '74* and *Other Tales of Suspense*

"Every novelist—aspiring and otherwise—should read Gary
Reilly's *Jeremy Bannister, Or the Ups and Downs of an Aspiring
Novelist*. The slender volume, with its chapter-per-page
format, is a sly and witty send-up of the writing life, with
Bannister's quest to become a 'big-shot novelist' full of the
painfully recognizable actions that defeat actual writing. The
book's laugh-out-loud moments vie with the heartache of
knowing Reilly's own published-novelist status came only
posthumously." - Gwen Florio, author of *Silent Hearts, Best
Laid Plans*, and the forthcoming *The Truth of It All*

"This might be Gary Reilly's funniest novel, and that's saying
something. It's also an excruciatingly accurate look at the
lengths to which writers will go to maintain a writerly self-
image while barely writing anything at all." - David Rea,
author, songwriter, and recording artist (*Nation of One, Sage
and Seer*)

"If there's an irony in this thinly veiled autobiography, it's
that a writer of Gary Reilly's great talent would have judged
his younger self so harshly. But Jeremy Bannister's endless
attempts to greet his destiny as a 'big-shot novelist' are by
turns pathetic, touching, thought provoking, and laugh-out-

loud hilarious. This lightning-fast read's strongest appeal will undoubtedly be to other writers—but outsiders and strivers of any stripe will recognize themselves in Jeremy Bannister, too. My favorite novel about an outsider author since Sam Savage's *Firmin*." - author and editor Keir Graff

"As a writer, Jeremy Bannister's plans make grasping at straws seem like a solid choice. Reilly puts us deep into his character's point of view and through Jeremy's hilarious fog of ineptitude, ignorance, and deep dedication I joyfully followed his journey to its end. If you want to be a writer, read this book and avoid everything in it. Or not." - Larry Barber, award-winning television writer and producer

"I love this book so much. I devoured it page after page like a bag of potato chips yet when I was finished, I felt I'd consumed a full, multi-course feast. There was no guilt from laughing at the clueless foolishness of the title character because I was clearly laughing at myself as a young, self-conscious, bumbling fool trying to escape "real" work and become an artist. With a near Hemingway economy of words, Gary Reilly pinned the tail on my existential donkey with amazing accuracy. Did this guy know me?" - Dan Piraro, creator of *Bizarro* and *Peyote Cowboy*

"*Jeremy Bannister* is for anyone who has dreamed of being a writer. Through Jeremy, Gary Reilly teaches us not to be afraid of rejection. You don't have a be a 'big-shot novelist,' just stay focused and keep writing." - J. Scott Simmons, documentary film producer

"A new book from an author we lost too soon, *Jeremy Bannister* is a delightfully resonant look into the life of a writer who just might be destined to do great things." - Wendy J. Fox, author of *If the Ice Had Held* and *What if We Were Somewhere Else*

By Gary Reilly:

The Asphalt Warrior Series
The Asphalt Warrior
Ticket to Hollywood
Heart of Darkness Club
Home for the Holidays
Doctor Lovebeads
Dark Night of the Soul
Pickup at Union Station
Devil's Night
Varmint Rumble

The Private Palmer Series:
The Enlisted Men's Club
The Detachment
The Discharge

Standalone Novels:
The Circumstantial Man
The Legend of Carl Draco

Jeremy Bannister, or The Ups and Downs of an Aspiring Novelist

Gary Reilly

Running Meter Press
Denver

Jeremy Bannister, or The Ups and Downs of an Aspiring Novelist

By Gary Reilly

Running Meter Press
Mancos, Colorado

Published by Running Meter Press
Mancos, Colorado
Publisher@RunningMeterPress.com

Cover art by Mike Keefe
Cover exterior and interior design by Jody Chapel

ISBN: 978-0-9909927-1-4
Library of Congress Control Number: 2021905496

First Edition 2021
Printed in the United States of America

Foreword

Beginning at age ten, Jeremy Bannister had one lifelong, all-consuming ambition—to become a "big-shot novelist." He started checking out books from the public library and envisioned himself as a rich and renowned literary giant. While his classmates played kickball, he would sit under an oak tree with an imaginary pencil and notebook, putting the finishing touches on a make-believe blockbuster.

One thing for sure, Jeremy was never going to work for a living, unlike his father who was employed at a laundromat.

As the years passed, he actually put a few words on paper—but not very many. Biding his time, he estimated that it would take him two years after high school to make it big. His dream was sidetracked with a U.S. Army draft notice and a year in a war zone. After his military service, he found it necessary to drive a cab to pay for food and a cheap room. A little bit of college, too.

Still, churning in his mind was the notion that destiny was on his side. He even considered changing his middle name to a more memorable moniker for the library bookshelves he was certain to inhabit for all of posterity. Jeremy Galbraith Bannister. Jeremy Truehart Bannister. Jeremy Fenimore Bannister.

Ultimately, he was able to start manuscripts with the support of a subscription to *Aspiring Writer Magazine*. He sent query letters to agents, sample chapters and outlines to publishers. One hundred percent of them were returned with terse rejection slips.

Still, Jeremy continued to dream.

Jeremy Bannister is the creation of another aspiring novelist—Gary Reilly. Gary created the comic nine-volume Asphalt Warrior series about, yes, another cab-driving, wannabe writer named Murph. He also authored a trilogy about Private Palmer's time before, during, and after the Vietnam War. So, too, did he write the stand-alone novels *The Circumstantial Man* and *The Legend of Carl Draco*.

Every one of those fourteen novels have been published by Running Meter Press beginning in 2012, a year after Gary's death. All have received rave reviews in *The Denver Post*, National Public

Radio, *Booklist* and stellar comments from writers Stewart O'Nan, Jeffery Deaver, and Ron Carlson (among many others). His books have been frequent finalists for The Colorado Book Awards. All were local bestsellers.

Jeremy Bannister, or The Ups and Downs of an Aspiring Novelist is now the fifteenth posthumous publication. It is not only a great read, but it comes in an arresting visual design—each chapter is exactly one paragraph long, all the same length.

Mark Stevens and I were close friends with Gary. We were aware of his incredible skills as a writer and of his steamer trunk full of unpublished novels. That's the sole reason we formed Running Meter Press—to finally put Gary Reilly's work out in the world.

But we have had tons of help along the way. We would like to thank three key members of the Running Meter Press team: editor Karen Haverkamp, who brings the highest standards to her work and ensures that Gary's manuscripts are publication-ready; book designer Jody Chapel, who has brought her creative touch and thoughtful eye to designing every title; and web designer Anita Austin, who keeps a snazzy online presence for Gary's works at www.theasphaltwarrior.com.

We would also like to thank all of Gary's extended friends and family who have supported the publication effort and the growing number of fans who are spreading the word about his talents. In addition, we'd like to thank two of Denver's fine independent bookstores, The Tattered Cover and BookBar. Both stores have given Gary space on their shelves and support in their hearts.

It is now time for you to get to know an earnest, young and, yes, aspiring writer. He's a bit like Don Quixote. Only our hero doesn't wield a lance. His weapon of choice is a number-two graphite pencil. And, later, a beat-up Smith Corona.

Ladies and gentlemen, meet Jeremy Bannister.

Mike Keefe
Running Meter Press
March 2021

Chapter 1

Jeremy Bannister decided he wanted to be a big-shot novelist when he was ten years old, the age at which his mother first allowed him to begin checking books out of the public library on his own. He was fascinated by the idea of writing famous books to earn money rather than working every day at a laundromat, as did his father. All through his grade-school years Jeremy gazed out the windows of his various classrooms and wondered what he was doing studying textbooks. "I should be living in New York City," he told himself. More than anything in the world, he wanted to become a big-shot novelist. He wanted it so badly that he even began pretending he already was one. During recess, while the other kids were playing kickball, he would sit under an oak tree at the edge of the playground, chewing idly on an imaginary pencil and gazing at an imaginary tablet on his knee and pretending that he was revising a great novel that would make him rich beyond his wildest dreams. Sometimes he would lift his chin and peer into the distance as though he were contemplating a complex and intriguing plot. He would nod slowly, pinch his index finger and thumb together, and wriggle his wrist as if jotting down an idea before it escaped his mind. All the other kids would laugh at him as he stared at his knee, and some of them would yell, "Look at the big-shot novelist!" Even as his face burned crimson with ire, Jeremy Bannister muttered to himself, "If only they knew. If . . . only . . . they . . . knew."

1

Chapter 2

When Jeremy was in eighth grade, the kid who lived across the street from him was given a set of barbells for his birthday. All of the other kids who lived in the neighborhood came over to watch him lift weights in his garage. Some of the big kids asked if they could try it out too, but the skinniest kids sneered among themselves at the whole concept of lifting weights. "I once read this article in a magazine about a weight lifter whose muscles got so big that he couldn't even bend his arms to comb his hair!" a skinny kid said. "Wow," another skinny kid said, "there's no way I'm ever gonna lift barbells. I sure wouldn't want to get that muscle-bound!" Jeremy Bannister was one of the skinny kids. He shook his head with disgust at the idea of having so many muscles that he couldn't even perform the simplest of human tasks. While the rest of the kids were lying on a bench huffing and puffing, Jeremy pointed at them and laughed with derision, and acted as if he was about to leave at any minute because he had many more interesting things to do with his valuable time. In truth, he too wanted to work out with the barbells. But that would be like publicly admitting that he was skinny and weak. So instead he pretended he was doing just fine without muscles. Let the weaklings build up their sorry bodies, he chortled inwardly as he left the garage and walked across the street. He went into his house and climbed the stairs to his bedroom, and got back to the more intellectual pursuit of pretending to revise a great novel.

Chapter 3

During high school Jeremy joined the football team. He was still skinny and weak, but his father made him do it. However, as a person who wanted to become a big-shot novelist, he had nothing but contempt for the idea of competitive sports. He truly doubted whether any of the loudmouth jocks on the football team had ever attempted to write an actual novel, much less read one as an extracurricular activity. The football team practiced every night after school, and Jeremy made a special point of staying out of the coach's way as much as possible. He would spend anywhere from ten to twenty minutes tying and retying his shoes, until the coach yelled at him to get off his duff. On the last day of the season, in a game that promised to give his high school the state championship, Jeremy was sent into the line during the last quarter. His team was ahead by three points, but the opposing team had the ball. It was third and goal. The center hiked the ball. The quarterback handed off to a fullback who came right at Jeremy. The fullback had a pug nose and buckteeth and weighed two hundred pounds. He had been held back two grades by his parents as well as his bad grades. He was gigantic. As he approached like a rocket, Jeremy suddenly grasped the pointlessness of high school sports. He got down on one knee and pretended to tie his bootlace. The kid dashed across the goal line and won the game. When Jeremy stood up, everybody booed him. But in his own mind, Jeremy Bannister had made his first artistic statement.

3

Chapter 4

Nobody at school would speak to Jeremy after the day of the big loss. That was fine with him. At night he would hide out in his bedroom while his humiliated father railed at him down in the living room. Jeremy could hear his voice rising above the sound of the TV. His mother didn't say anything about it, but Jeremy knew what she was thinking: you made your father yell again. Jeremy lay on his bed and dreamed about the future when he would become a big-shot novelist. One day as Jeremy was walking home from school, he saw a typewriter for sale in the window of a pawn shop. He walked up to the window and stared at the machine. It was a Smith Corona. Jeremy felt as if the typewriter was beckoning to him. He decided the time had finally come to begin preparing himself for his successful writing career. He went in and bought the typewriter for two dollars and took it home, sneaking in the back door so his father wouldn't see it. He did realize that he would not become a big-shot novelist right away and calculated that it would probably take him at least two years after he got out of high school. This he was willing to admit to himself. It would take a lot of hard work, and probably a few unavoidable setbacks. He would sweat and strain, and then the day would come when he would be hailed by the critics. He wrote a short story that night, the very first and best story he had ever written. Then he lit a candle and burned the story to a crisp. Jeremy Bannister had made his second artistic statement.

Chapter 5

Jeremy was secretly in love with one of the girls in his senior class. Her name was Dolores. Jeremy had an overwhelming urge to date her, even though he had never been on a date before. But he felt that, as an aspiring big-shot novelist, it was time to get his feet wet because insights into the mysteries of romance would surely play a large role in his life as a writer. He had read a few Norman Mailer books already, so he knew that sooner or later he would have to start writing about the opposite sex. Even though no one at school was speaking to him, he managed to finagle a date with Dolores, who also had never been on a date. Jeremy talked his mother into talking his father into letting him have the car. His father railed for a while but finally relented, gave him the keys, and told him to keep it between the telephone poles. Jeremy didn't know what he meant by that, and was afraid to ask. After the movie, Jeremy and Dolores parked out at "the lake" where all the teens parked. Jeremy was a little bit apprehensive about "making a move" for the first time in his life, but Dolores brought his petty worries to an end by grabbing him by the lapels and kissing him swiftly on the lips. Jeremy held on tightly to the steering wheel. After a moment of bafflement, he realized her tongue was inside his mouth. "Do you love me?" Dolores began whispering softly. Trying to remember everything he could from both the fiction and nonfiction of Norman Mailer, Jeremy pulled his head back and replied, "Perhaps."

Chapter 6

Jeremy and Dolores became a hot item at school for a week. As the pair walked down the hallways holding hands between classes, girls would glance out of the corners of their eyes and whisper secret things and giggle, then hide their faces behind their textbooks. None of the jocks whispered though. They made loud wisecracks as the pair walked by. One afternoon a bunch of jocks cornered Jeremy in the senior parking lot and started roughing him up. At first he thought they were jealous of him and Dolores, but he finally realized that they were still upset about the football game. "Where did you learn to catch, creep?" some of them snarled. Others snarled, "Don't you have any school spirit?" Jeremy said nothing, waiting for them to let him go, which he knew they would eventually have to do or else get in trouble. Each evening Jeremy would escort Dolores to her house. Her parents never seemed to be home, which struck him as odd. Dolores would invite him into the den, where she would drag him onto the couch and kiss him and whisper, "Do you love me?" After five days of this, Jeremy decided to explain that while love would someday play a major role in his life, he was not ready to fall in love with any particular girl just yet. "I plan on becoming a big-shot novelist someday, and it will probably take me at least two—" But that's as far as he got before Dolores erupted into violent tears and screamed at him to get out. After that, nobody at all spoke to him during or after school.

Chapter 7

Jeremy's high school graduation ceremony was to be held at the auditorium downtown on the first of June, but on that day Jeremy was nowhere to be seen. He had decided to stay home in order to demonstrate to everyone his contempt for The System. "Frickum," he said aloud as he lay on his bed. Neither of his parents made an inquiry as to why he wasn't at the graduation ceremony. They hadn't made any plans to attend it, and probably had other things on their minds. Jeremy stared at the ceiling, smiling inwardly and imagining the howls of outrage that would pour forth from the doors of the auditorium at the precise moment when the school administrators discovered to their utter dismay that Jeremy had snubbed the ceremony. The principal would storm around the stage demanding explanations and making empty threats. The teachers would all be in a tizzy. Most of the students would be stunned because none of them had ever experienced such stark rebellion before. The vivid imagery of this scene filled Jeremy with a sweaty fear alloyed with unbearable excitement. When his mother called him down to dinner he told her that he was too sick to eat, which he was in a way, even though he was lying. Around six o'clock that evening, tired of showing his contempt, Jeremy finally crawled out of bed and went downstairs. He ate some cold leftovers, then stepped out onto the front porch and saw his diploma lying out on the lawn. How it had gotten there he did not know. It was a mystery that was never to be solved.

7

Chapter 8

In early June, Jeremy turned eighteen and moved out of his house after his parents told him to leave. He answered a want ad and was quickly hired to be an assistant refrigerator mover. His job would be to ride shotgun in a delivery truck. His weekly pay would allow him to rent a cheap apartment within walking distance of the warehouse. Proud to be out in the world on his own, Jeremy called upon his newfound maturity and worked out a household budget that involved a lot of cans of spaghetti. As he ate his first meal in his new apartment, he dreamed of the day when he would become a rich big-shot novelist, and would find himself eating cans of caviar while living in a mansion that had a swimming pool and a garage large enough for as many cars as he could afford. But right now he would concentrate on living frugally and eating cheaply. It was how he imagined a bohemian novelist in New York City would live, a person who put off getting rich so that he could concentrate on producing great art in a garret, which was the place where great art normally came from. Jeremy would have preferred to move to New York City. However, from what little he knew about the East Coast, it struck him as too expensive. But he believed that if he lived like a struggling artist, it would help to keep him on the right track toward getting published in the future. From everything he had read about novelists who had made it to the top of the literary world long before him, suffering seemed to be the key.

Chapter 9

Each morning Jeremy rolled out of bed eager to make his way in the world. He felt that working alongside simple blue-collar workers would give him insights into the lower classes that would be invaluable to an aspiring novelist. Jeremy's own father managed a laundromat but always wore a clean white shirt to work, which, in Jeremy's opinion, elevated his family above the lower classes—although technically he had to admit that he was from the lower middle classes as opposed to being a regular middle-class person. He felt a little bit embarrassed to be from a higher social scale than his fellow workers, but he swore to himself that he would treat them as equally as he could. He felt that there were many things the lower classes would be able to teach him about life. The people in the lower classes were industrious and boisterous. They laughed heartily. They exulted in the drudgery of endless labor. They knew the secret of life, which they were loath to reveal to the white-collar workers of the world. On his first day on the job, Jeremy was told to help the driver load a refrigerator onto the rear of the delivery truck. It was the hardest labor that Jeremy had ever performed, and after the refrigerator was secured with ropes, his back was aching. As the driver guided the big truck along a boulevard, Jeremy worked up his courage and confessed that he intended to become a big-shot novelist someday. The driver, a fifty-year-old man, glanced over at Jeremy and said, "I nebber read books. I watch teebee."

Chapter 10

After Jeremy lost the delivery job for being too weak to move large appliances, he spent a week perusing want ads and wallowing in the luxury of being an unemployed writer. He had just enough money saved to carry him through to the next payday, should such a thing arrive. Every day he would stroll lazily down to the corner and purchase a newspaper from a box. On the way back to his apartment he would often stop and stare at the people who had outside jobs, such as construction workers. Jeremy would smile to himself, knowing that the day would eventually come when he could take these very same walks as a wealthy writer. When he got back to his place he would sit down and open the newspaper. He would first read the comics and the letters to the editor, then he would turn over to the want ads. He read the ads in alphabetical order, staying up late into the night. He would sleep until noon the next day, eat a can of spaghetti, then go out and buy another newspaper. He eventually discovered that new jobs were not necessarily offered on each successive day. They always seemed to be the same jobs that he was not qualified to apply for, or else did not want to apply for because they looked too hard. If only he knew how to be an accountant, he mused to himself aloud one evening. If only he was trained as a respiratory therapist. There were tons of entry-level jobs available for qualified personnel, but he didn't find any job openings for apprentice novelists. He pondered this strange truth far into the night.

Chapter 11

Even though Jeremy planned to become a novelist, he decided that the best way to begin his career would be to write short stories. Once he got pretty good at that, he would then move on up to the novel. He wanted to take things one step at a time. He had another motive though, and that was to make some fast money by selling his short stories to fantasy magazines, which eventually would help to support his novel writing. He had never written a fantasy story before, but he had always prided himself on his vivid imagination. Surely anybody who thought the way he did would have little trouble writing stories about rocket ships or elves. He wrote one short story per day, and mailed it out the next day. That year he received seven rejection slips per week, as well as one intriguing note from an editor advising him to include a return envelope with each story. He jotted this hot tip down in a notebook and felt that he was learning the secret ins and outs of the publishing world. During that year he held a variety of jobs. He worked as a janitor, a hamburger cook, a car-wash attendant, a mail-room clerk, an assistant electrician, an assistant linoleum layer, an assistant groundskeeper, an egg inspector, a shag boy, and a ditchdigger. He was fired from all of these jobs for the same reason. Then one evening it occurred to him that he ought to begin writing his first novel. He was struck by the uniqueness of this notion. It seemed like a logical step in becoming a big-shot novelist. He decided to give it a trial run.

Chapter 12

The very next day Jeremy Bannister was drafted. On the one hand, he was a bit disappointed that he would not be able to dive right into his novel. On the other hand, he felt that two years in the army would add vast knowledge to draw upon whenever he did get around to starting his novel. He knew that many famous authors had gotten their start in the writing game by describing the horrors they had seen in war, even if they made up the worst parts. Before being sworn in to the army, he watched a lot of war movies on TV so that he could learn the ins and outs of the army. He wanted to be in the know when it came to obeying orders like a robot. On the first day of basic training, a drill sergeant inspected the men as they stood at attention in their barracks. The sergeant opened Jeremy's wall locker and found it stuffed with books. "Where in the living hell is your authorized goddamn equipment?" he barked. Jeremy smiled at the sergeant with pity and informed him that there wasn't enough room in the locker for his books, so he had returned his military equipment to the supply room. "What?" the sergeant screamed. Jeremy took a few moments to explain that he intended to use his time in the army wisely by reading as many great novels as he could because he intended to become a big-shot novelist someday. "A big-shit novelist?" the drill sergeant screamed while Jeremy performed twenty push-ups. After that, Jeremy's fellow trainees began referring to him as "The Big-Shit Novelist."

Chapter 13

After Jeremy got out of basic training, he was sent to infantry school to learn how to be a grunt. Some of his basic training buddies ended up with him, so his new nickname stuck and was eventually picked up by the new drill sergeants who used it without even knowing what it meant. After another eight weeks, Jeremy was shipped overseas to the war. Which war doesn't really matter, for are not all wars the same? None of his training buddies had gotten assigned to his combat unit, so he was never again referred to as "The Big-Shit Novelist" to his face. After he got to the war, he thought about sending Dolores a Dear John letter. He seemed to recall that type of letter being written by soldiers in the movies. But he was afraid that Dolores was probably still mad at him and might not write back. A week after he arrived at his unit, he was sent to the front lines and was ordered to get into a foxhole. His new buddies told him to get his damn head down and start shooting at the enemy. Kneeling in the mud, Jeremy suddenly was overwhelmed by the absurdity of war. "I shall not shoot at strangers just because the government tells me to," he snarled inwardly. Instead, he decided to tell his buddies about his lifelong plans to become a big-shot novelist. "I am fully aware that the odds of my success in the writing game are slim. However, I feel that if a person doesn't give something an honest try, he definitely will never make it." None of his new buddies responded. None of them seemed to even be moving.

Chapter 14

After Jeremy got out of the army, he decided not to get a job, even though he felt that manual labor was a plus for a writer who might want to reveal the truth about the evils of big business. But he was too tired from being in the army, so he decided to go to college on the G.I. Bill, which would pay all of his expenses. He also had a lot of money saved up because there hadn't been much to buy in the war. He applied to the state university and found out that he had to take an SAT test, which he took at his old high school. Even though he had been through a war, he was still afraid that his old principal might see him and start asking pointed questions. Jeremy passed the test and was eventually accepted at State U. He took a bus to the university, where he rented an upstairs apartment in a house. He told his landlady that he was a veteran attending school on the G.I. Bill and that his major was going to be English. With all the vast knowledge of the English language that he would acquire, he felt he would have a leg up over the rest of the writers in America. But first he had to take a writing proficiency test. It seemed simple enough to him, but he was later told that he would have to attend a basic English course, which was referred to by the student body as "Dumb-Dumb English." Infuriated, Jeremy thought about dropping out. But his first $300 check from the government arrived, so he decided to put his rebellion on temporary hold. "Frickum," he said to himself. He . . . would . . . show . . . them.

14

Chapter 15

During his first week of school Jeremy had a meeting with his assigned student advisor. The man told him that the only viable career for an English major after graduation was to become an English teacher. Jeremy smirked to himself, keeping secret the fact that he was using college merely as a stepping-stone to becoming a big-shot novelist. He had no intention of learning how to teach English. He would devote the next four years to learning how to write novels, drawing upon all of the valuable information that he would receive from the fiction he would study in his English classes. Immediately upon graduation he would begin writing best-selling novels. But after taking a class involving *The Norton Anthology*, Jeremy got an idea. He could use his education to his advantage! Why not write an epic poem? Nobody else seemed to be writing epic poems nowadays. The field appeared to be wide open. He would probably have very little competition. He might even be able to carve out a niche for himself. And if his epic poem made a big enough splash in the academic world, perhaps he would be awarded an honorary degree from the English department, and might be offered a teaching job. He threw himself into the project to the detriment of his other studies and spent two weeks drawing upon all the powers of his creative imagination, as well as models in *The Norton Anthology*. Inspired by *Beowulf, Paradise Lost*, and Alexander Pope, he wrote an epic poem set in the third century BC. It was twenty thousand words long.

15

Chapter 16

One afternoon Jeremy was sauntering home from an English class in which he had just received an A for an essay on Alexander Pope. In every English course he was taking, he had received an A on every single essay. He had also turned out to be the top student in his Dumb-Dumb English class. He was immensely proud of this achievement and imagined that when the New York publishers became aware of this they would not only be quite impressed, but he himself would have an "in" with the editors. He imagined the editors seated in their offices in New York City with pipes clenched between their teeth, looking over his impressive resume and nodding to themselves. They might even decide to phone him personally to discuss his budding writing career. When he got back home he found a familiar manila envelope in his mailbox. Slightly perplexed, he carried the envelope up to his apartment and opened it. He discovered his epic poem inside it. Attached to it was a rejection slip. Jeremy peered into the envelope thinking that perhaps some sort of an error had been made at the publishing house where he had submitted the poem two weeks ago. He had been expecting an acceptance slip, not a rejection slip. He didn't know what to think. He quickly leafed through the pages to see if an editor might possibly have scribbled an explanation for the quick return of the poem, but there were no scribbles to be found. Jeremy frowned with confusion. Then he came to the startling conclusion that his poem had been rejected.

Chapter 17

The autumn days drifted by. Jeremy did not go to any of his classes. He lay on his couch staring bleakly at the rejection slip, which he had scotch-taped to the wall above him. "Why?" he whispered. "Why?" For two weeks he had been wallowing in a fantasy that his epic poem would be accepted by the publisher and his entire life would be changed. Not only would he achieve a certain amount of local fame and notoriety, but money would begin rolling in. Readers from around the world, especially English professors, would be writing to his publishing house heaping praise on this unknown author and demanding to see more of his work. Outside, the wind blew. Autumn leaves were cascading from the trees. Jeremy pondered the fact that it had been three years since he had graduated from high school. His original intention had been to become a big-shot novelist within two years after high school, and three already had passed. Of course, a year ago he was in the war, so he hardly could have been expected to write anything. Certainly, the literary critics would have to take this fact into consideration. He sat up and did some quick mental arithmetic. "If I subtract my two years in the army from the past three years, that means I still have one year left to attain my goal of becoming a big-shot novelist!" Reinvigorated with ambition, he dashed to his typewriter and rolled a blank sheet of paper through the platen. He sat there staring at the keys excitedly. After a while he began cracking his knuckles and fidgeting.

Chapter 18

Jeremy was called into his advisor's office one week later and was asked why he had not been attending his classes. Jeremy wanted to tell the advisor that he had received his worst rejection slip ever and felt that he had earned the right to heap scorn upon the trivial demands of scholarship. But as the excuse took form in his brain, it began to seem sort of weak. In fact, it seemed not unlike the plots of many short stories that he had abandoned. "I've been kind of sick," he lied. His advisor frowned at him with suspicion and asked if he drank much alcohol. "I tried it once in the army," Jeremy said. That was where he had gotten drunk for the first time in his life. It was also the last time, to date. His advisor then sent him to the campus clinic, where a doctor gave him a physical and asked him to describe the symptoms of his illness. Having never been sick in his life, Jeremy was completely out of his element when it came to lying to a doctor. He usually felt out of his element when it came to lying. He decided to tell the doctor that he just felt out of sorts. The doctor frowned with suspicion, then told him to come back if any symptoms happened to re-erupt. Jeremy attended all of his classes the following week, experiencing a sweaty fear that his advisor would receive a suspicious report from the physician and Jeremy would have to fabricate new lies. But the only consequence was a remark from an English professor who said he was pleased that Mr. Bannister at last had decided to grace the classroom with his presence.

18

Chapter 19

While shopping for spaghetti at the supermarket one afternoon, Jeremy spotted a magazine titled *Aspiring Writer Magazine*. He had never seen this periodical in the campus bookstore, so he stopped to peruse it. His hair almost stood on end when he discovered what it was. The magazine was filled with tips for aspiring writers! He had never known that such a magazine existed anywhere in the world. He felt as if he had uncovered a secret treasure trove that nobody else knew about. He put the magazine into his shopping cart, then stocked up on canned spaghetti. However, when he went up to the cashier to pay for his grocery items he suddenly became overwhelmed by a nagging sense of embarrassment. While he had never shied away from telling acquaintances about his writing ambitions, the idea of a store cashier knowing exactly what he was up to filled him with apprehension. He lifted the magazine from his cart as he got in line and acted like he was merely perusing a periodical that he had grabbed from a nearby rack and had no idea what was in it. As the cashier began ringing up the items, Jeremy surreptitiously set the magazine next to his cans, then watched the woman out of the corner of his eye and tried hard to control his facial expression. He began mentally concocting some sort of explanation for the presence of the magazine and hoping that the cashier would not make a pointed remark about his writing ambitions. He felt nearly prostrate with relief when the woman finally said, "Six ninety-two."

Chapter 20

During his perusal of *Aspiring Writer Magazine* that night, Jeremy came across an intriguing article that advised beginning writers to study the marketplace in order to learn what the editors wanted. This sounded like a viable idea. Jeremy had never approached his writing from this angle before. He mostly just tried to think up stuff on his own. He felt a shiver of joy pass through him, knowing that he was receiving hot tips from the pros. It was really too late at night to go study the marketplace, so he considered the fact that horror novels had come into popular vogue of late. For one moment he felt elated. He had purchased this magazine only a few hours ago, and already he was incorporating some of its advice. He decided to go ahead and write a horror novel. He got up from the couch and went to his typewriter, rolled a sheet of blank paper through the platen, and stared at it. He tried to think of the most horrifying thing he could possibly imagine. The closest he came was his first date with Dolores. While this didn't seem like the sort of incident that book publishers would be looking for, he suddenly got an idea for a plot. Suppose a young man was strolling through a cemetery late at night when a female corpse burst out of a grave, grabbed him by the lapels, kissed him, and whispered, "Do you love me?" Jeremy quickly typed up this scene, then spent the rest of the week trying to think up some kind of a plot to go along with it. But it seemed like the opening scene had pretty much said it all.

Chapter 21

Jeremy went back to perusing his copy of *Aspiring Writer Magazine*, looking for any other hot tips that might help him kick-start his writing career. He found a classified-ads section near the back. A lot of schools devoted strictly to writing were advertised there, and he wondered if he should have gone to one of those places instead of to college. He was then amazed to find dozens of ads posted by literary agents who said they were willing to read unsolicited manuscripts for a small fee. He was electrified by the idea that actual agents in New York City could be reading his stories within a week, and some of them charged only thirty dollars! Jeremy set the magazine aside and calculated how many unpublished manuscripts he had, and how many were polished enough to send to agents. Then he compared that to how much money he would earn if the agents sold only half of his short stories. He came to the irrefutable conclusion that if he submitted ten stories to ten of these agents, he would ultimately come out on top financially, which had always been his dream. He spent the next five days retyping clean copies of his stories. He stuffed ten manuscripts into ten envelopes along with ten thirty-dollar checks. He walked to a nearby post office and mailed the stories to ten agents. Within two weeks all of his manuscripts came back with notes informing him that his stories had been deemed unsaleable. When he received his next $300 check from the government, he felt as if he was holding smoke in his hands.

Chapter 22

One afternoon toward the end of autumn, as he was sauntering home from another class where he had just received another A, Jeremy saw his landlady standing on the driveway. "I have a proposition for you," she said with a smile. Jeremy was immediately filled with apprehension. In his entire lifetime nobody had ever offered him a proposition that ultimately worked in his favor. He thought about telling her that he had a pressing engagement and didn't have time to talk, but he just stood there fidgeting anxiously. "I would be willing to lower your monthly rent if you were to take on the responsibility of raking up all the fallen leaves, and shoveling the snow in the winter, and mowing the lawn in the spring," the woman said. "It's been an awful lot of work to take care of this old house all by myself ever since my husband passed on." Jeremy suddenly felt like an escaped convict trapped by a searchlight. He hadn't done any manual labor since he had gotten out of the army. It was his lifelong plan never to do any manual labor. "I'll have to think about it," he stuttered. He hurried up into his apartment and locked the door shut. He stood motionless for an hour, afraid to make any sound for fear it would cause his landlady to think of him. How could his landlady not understand that his rent was already free, since the G.I. Bill was paying for all of his school expenses? Didn't she have any sense of logic? Jeremy spent the rest of his freshman year successfully avoiding his landlady, and paying his rent by mail.

Chapter 23

When the next issue of *Aspiring Writer Magazine* was scheduled to appear on the stands, Jeremy went to the store and bought a month's worth of spaghetti, hoping that the vast number of cans would distract the cashier from the presence of the magazine. His ruse worked rather well, and that night he perused an article about pseudonyms. He began to reflect on the fact that many old-time writers had three names. Edgar Allan Poe did. So did John Greenleaf Whittier. He began to wonder if his manuscripts might be more saleable if he employed three names. It seemed to him that this would appear more professional, and that the editors might be swayed by the seriousness with which he took his reputation. Whenever he saw a new book written by a contemporary novelist who had three names, he was impressed by how important the book probably was. His own middle name was Tyke, so he decided to come up with a brand-new middle name. After all, pseudonyms were a somewhat common practice in the industry, so he certainly would not get into any sort of legal trouble if he used one, although he might have to get his name changed in court just to cover his ass. He sat down at his typewriter and toyed with various pseudonyms, such as Jeremy Armstrong Bannister, or Jeremy Carruthers Bannister, or Jeremy Erikson Bannister, or Jeremy Huntington Bannister, or Jeremy Galbraith Bannister, or Jeremy Donaldson Bannister, hoping to come up with a pseudonym that held a certain elegant resonance.

Chapter 24

Jeremy Hames Bannister. Jeremy Jackson Bannister. Jeremy Northdale Bannister. Jeremy Guggenheim Bannister. Jeremy Fandango Bannister. Jeremy Boomer Bannister. Jeremy Hemingway Bannister. Jeremy Broadway Bannister. Jeremy Masterman Bannister. Jeremy Truehart Bannister. Jeremy Swashbuckler Bannister. Jeremy The Conqueror Bannister. Jeremy Bullfinch Bannister. Jeremy Staircase Bannister. Jeremy Embarcadero Bannister. Jeremy X. Bannister. Jeremy Rafe Bannister. Jeremy Vorthaven Bannister. Jeremy Buckminster Bannister. Jeremy Westminster Bannister. Jeremy The Kid Bannister. Jeremy Hondo Bannister. Jeremy Bud Bannister. Jeremy The Greek Bannister. Jeremy Boom-Boom Bannister. Jeremy Hepburn Bannister. Jeremy Greenleaf Bannister. Jeremy The Man Bannister. Jeremy Nighthawk Bannister. Jeremy Foxfire Bannister. Jeremy Nimrod Bannister. Jeremy Big Danny Bannister. Jeremy Longworth Bannister. Jeremy Motown Bannister. Jeremy Spats Bannister. Jeremy Stroheim Bannister. Jeremy von Stroheim Bannister. Jeremy Armbrewster Bannister. Jeremy Boswell Bannister. Jeremy Orwell Bannister. Jeremy Burgess Bannister. Jeremy von Ribbentroff Bannister. Jeremy von Zell Bannister. Jeremy Deacon Bannister. Jeremy Studs Bannister. Jeremy Lofton Bannister. Jeremy Night Train Bannister. Jeremy Fennimore Bannister. Jeremy Rambling Bannister. Jeremy Stuart Bannister. Jeremy Psycho Bannister. Jeremy Big-Shot Bannister.

Three weeks later, a self-addressed stamped envelope addressed to Jeremy Fontaine Bannister arrived at his apartment with a rejection slip. Jeremy had spent the past three weeks wallowing in a fantasy that an editor in New York City might not only accept his story but would even comment upon the elegance of his middle name. Now he wondered if he ought to have sent the short story out at all. Suppose he was to get published someday but did not utilize his new middle name, and this particular editor realized that he had been duped? Who knows? The Word might get out that a fraud was working publishers' row. In order to take his mind off his dread, Jeremy started leafing through his copy of *Aspiring Writer Magazine* looking for another tip that might help him get published. He wanted to buy the latest issue of the magazine but felt that his facial expression might reveal to a cashier that he had a lot of rejection slips. Was it possible that there might be a small grocery store where the lower classes bought their magazines and no cashier would recognize him? But he felt that he would have trouble controlling his facial expression even among the lower classes. He considered the idea of sending away for a yearlong subscription to the magazine, but what if his landlady saw it and began asking pointed questions? She might think he was desperate for money, and toss him out. A subscription to the magazine could ruin everything. His mind began to spin. He had never suspected that the writing life would be such a tough row to hoe.

Chapter 26

When the school year came to an end, Jeremy packed all of his belongings into his two suitcases, then went looking for his landlady, whom he had not seen in seven months. He found her standing in the front yard trying to pull-start a lawnmower. He set his suitcases down next to a can of gasoline and smiled at her, and told her that he was looking forward to renting the apartment next autumn. His landlady told him that a female student already had given her a deposit on the apartment, so he would have to find another place to live. "I thought maybe you had died," she remarked. Jeremy couldn't tell if she was joking, and he realized now that he should not have gone out of his way to avoid his landlady throughout the year. He should have told her the truth about the fact that he didn't need any reduction in his rent. But he had never had much luck with telling anybody the truth. He had always found that it was better to say nothing at all, or lie. But that didn't matter anymore. He had another problem to face up to. He had to find a summer job because he didn't have much money. He thought of asking his parents if he could live with them but gave up on that idea as soon as it formed in his brain. His father knew that Jeremy wanted to become a big-shot novelist someday, and had told him to stop making all that goddamned racket at night with his goddamned typewriter. Jeremy's long-range plan was to do a lot of writing in the evenings this summer, now that he didn't have any homework to distract him.

Chapter 27

Jeremy took a bus to his hometown, and during the ride he used his time trying to decide what to do about work. He had never had much luck keeping a job, but he hoped he could keep one for at least three months. That would be a new record for him, not counting the army. When he arrived at the bus terminal, he carried his suitcases out to the curb and got into a Checker cab. He asked the driver to take him to the nearest employment agency. The driver turned on the meter and pulled away from the curb. Jeremy stared at the back of the man's head for a while, then decided to strike up a conversation. Taxi driving intrigued him. What strange lives these knights of the road must live. He wondered if they had apartments or if they lived inside their taxis. And did they earn enough money, or did they moonlight doing other jobs? Jeremy cleared his throat and informed the man that he was attending school at State University majoring in English, then modestly added that he intended to someday become a big-shot novelist. The cab driver glanced at him and said, to Jeremy's amazement, that he himself had once tried to become a novelist. When Jeremy asked if the driver had ever gotten anything published, the man started laughing, and inexplicably beeped his horn. Since the driver was the first "real" person that Jeremy had ever met who had tried to write novels, he asked if the man knew of any writing groups he might join in order to share his work with other aspiring novelists. "Try Yellow Cab," the driver said.

Chapter 28

To Jeremy's horror, the only job that the employment agency had for him was assistant refrigerator mover at the same company that he had worked for when he was eighteen. There were no other job openings in the entire city that he was qualified for. If he had not been broke, if he had been trained in respiratory therapy, Jeremy would have turned down the job. But he was beginning to feel a little bit hungry, even though he assumed, thanks to a required Psych 101 class he had taken, that this was merely psychosomatic. When he arrived at the company, he discovered that the very same people who had worked there four years ago were still working there. Even the truck driver was the same fifty-year-old man, though now fifty-four. Were it not for the fact that nobody remembered him, he would have felt foolish. Instead he felt as if he was having a creepy dream. On his first morning on the job, Jeremy discovered to his further horror that he was capable of moving heavy appliances. At some point during the past four years, he had miraculously gotten stronger. It was probably all of those goddamn army push-ups, he groused to himself. He deliberately did not mention to anyone that he had already worked at this place, and that he had been fired the first time. Every night he came home from work totally exhausted. His strength seemed to last only a day. Throughout June, July, and August of that summer, he was incapable of typing a single word of prose fiction. He barely even had the strength to heat up a can of spaghetti.

Chapter 29

When August finally came to an end, Jeremy went to the foreman and told him that he was quitting his job and going back to college. He expected the foreman to get mad and start a ruckus, but the foreman just nodded and went into the lavatory. Jeremy hurried back to his apartment and packed, then took a bus up to State U. Unfortunately, he arrived one day before classes were scheduled to begin, and when he started looking for an apartment he was dismayed to discover that every apartment in town already seemed to be rented. Desperate for a place to live, he used some of the money he had earned as a refrigerator mover to rent a seedy hotel room in a run-down part of town. He then went over to the university and informed the VA rep of his change of address. The rent on his room was sixty dollars a week, and he quickly deduced that he would be able to live here for four weeks on each VA check, assuming he did not eat more than sixty dollars' worth of food per month. Since this came to two dollars per day for all of his meals, he calculated that things would be touch and go for the next nine months. On his first night in his new room he stood looking around. The room contained a bed, a closet, a chest of drawers, and a sink. The bathroom was down the hall. He began to get the ominous feeling that he was not entirely in control of his life. But he tried to cheer himself up by reminding himself that living like a bohemian was part and parcel of becoming a serious novelist. "At least I'm suffering," he reflected.

Chapter 30

During the second week of Jeremy's sophomore year, he was sitting in a required American history class judiciously nibbling on cheese and crackers when he heard a student informing another student that one of his roommates had dropped out of school in order to get married. Making an unprecedented and frantic move, Jeremy leaned toward the first student and inquired as to whether he was looking for another roommate. He was so desperate to find a way to move out of his hotel room that he even forgot to control his facial expression. The student turned slowly around in his chair and looked Jeremy up and down, then he nodded. Apparently he did not find anything in Jeremy's demeanor that might cause him concern. His heart pounding, Jeremy explained that he was living in a hotel room and was looking for a less expensive place to live. The man introduced himself as "Speed" and said he lived in a duplex with two roommates, and that if Jeremy moved in, the shared rent among the four of them would come to seventy dollars apiece each month. Jeremy felt his eyes light up. He had no control over this, but he didn't want any anyway. This sounded like an incredibly good deal. Speed gave Jeremy his address and told him to drop by later on in the evening. Forgetting about his other classes, Jeremy hurried back to his seedy room and packed all of his belongings into his two suitcases. When he was finished he went down to the bathroom, stood in front of the mirror, and practiced looking normal.

Chapter 31

Jeremy was concerned that if he took a cab to Speed's place it might cost him half a week's rent. But he was so desperate to get out of the hotel that he was almost willing to risk all of his money. He called the local branch of Yellow Cab. When a taxi arrived he brought both suitcases with him, hoping for the best. He rode in the backseat of the cab with his typewriter on his lap. When he arrived at Speed's duplex, he could hear raucous music coming from inside. He carried all of his worldly possessions with him up to the porch and set them at his feet. He stood in front of the door for a few moments and tried hard to control his facial expression. Then he knocked a few times. The door flew open and a wild-eyed young man holding a can of beer hollered, "Where's the keg?" Jeremy quickly explained that he was not from a liquor store but had come here to see Speed, and to talk about filling the vacancy. "Hey, Speed!" the young man hollered. Then he told Jeremy to come on inside. "Where's the keg?" two voices hollered as Jeremy walked in. Speed was lying spread-eagled on the floor in front of two stereo speakers, but he recognized Jeremy and crawled up off the floor and introduced his friends, Joe and Jock, who stood nodding their heads to the beat of the music. "Do you have seventy dollars?" Jock hollered above the noisy music. Jeremy nodded. "He's in!" Jock barked, then said, "Do you like to drink beer?" Jeremy started to shrug with indifference, but then quickly sizing things up, he nodded enthusiastically.

31

Chapter 32

After the music was turned down, Jeremy told his new roommates a little bit about himself. Hoping to reassure them that they had not invited a loser into their midst, he explained that he was an English major and intended to become a big-shot novelist someday. "Hey, we know a guy who wants to be a novelist too!" Jock shouted. "Is that right?" Jeremy said, interested in meeting someone with whom he might be able to share his work. "Yeah. His name's Bayler. He was our last roommate. He dropped out because he had to get married!" Joe, Jock, and Speed started laughing and punching each other on the shoulders. It was only now that it occurred to Jeremy that he was older than his roommates, who were the same age he had been when he was in the war learning the truth about that old whore Death, which was what Ernest Hemingway called death, according to one of his English teachers. Joe and Jock ran to the refrigerator and began pulling out cans of beer. They handed a brew to Jeremy, who decided he might enjoy living in this environment. After each of them had drunk four or five cans of beer apiece, Jeremy's roommates showed him to his room. It had a bed, a closet, a chest of drawers, no sink, and the bathroom was down the hall. But at least he did have his own desk. Jeremy unpacked and set up his typewriter, and sat down in order to capture in ink his feelings about this change in his fortunes. But his new roommates came in and made him drink more beer, so he didn't get any writing done that night.

Chapter 33

Jeremy had never been much of a beer drinker. He had gotten drunk only one time before in his life, and that was an experience he preferred to forget. The experience had taken place toward the end of basic training and came about as a result of informing his buddies that he had never had sex before in his life. It had taken place during a bull session when all of the GIs were polishing their combat boots and bragging about their conquests of women. When the trainees had finished describing their conquests in detail, one of them asked Jeremy about his knowledge of nooky, since he was the only one who hadn't spoken during the bull session. Jeremy shyly admitted that he was probably the only virgin in the entire US Army. This caused so many hoots of derision that a group of men decided to take "The Big-Shit Novelist" to town and get him laid come next furlough. Jeremy was a little bit leery about this plan, but he finally decided that since unbridled sex did play a major role in many novels, especially the novels of Norman Mailer, he ought to go along with his buddies if only for the sake of art. The experience more or less ended in a hotel room in the nearby army town where Jeremy found himself throwing up in the presence of a woman whom he had met only a minute earlier. She made his drunk friends pay anyway, then tossed all of them out. During the entirety of his sophomore year, Jeremy experienced a kind of perpetual déjà vu involving beer and vomit, although it did not seem to involve any women.

33

Chapter 34

Jeremy's sophomore year in college was destined to be the toughest year of all, what with balancing a full load of courses and partying every night. He'd never written anything while drunk before, and found it to be exceptionally challenging. But he took heart in the irrefutable fact that many famous American novelists produced great art while drunk. At the end of that year, without having produced one single coherent word of fiction, Jeremy got onto a bus hungover and rode back home. He was disappointed that he had not been able to get started on a novel. He'd barely been able to start theme papers, and had finished most of them during lulls in keggers. Carrying his suitcases outside the bus terminal, he climbed into the first cab in line and found the exact same driver who had taken him to the employment agency one year earlier. Is my whole life going to be a perpetual series of déjà vus? Jeremy asked himself as they headed for the agency. When they arrived, Jeremy suddenly found himself unable to get out of the taxi. He knew that there was only one job waiting for him in the entire city. The driver turned around to see what was taking so long. Jeremy gazed at him with a look that must have said many significant things to him, for the driver said, "I remember you, pal. You once told me you wanted to become a big-shot novelist." Jeremy nodded. "I've seen that look on other writers' faces," the driver said. Then he drove Jeremy across town to the Yellow Cab employment office. "Time to join the writers' group."

34

Chapter 35

Although Jeremy was a little bit concerned about the probability of getting robbed at gunpoint someday, his instinctual hesitation about being a cab driver was counterbalanced by the probability of hauling heavy appliances. So he went ahead and applied for a job as a Yellow Cab driver. He passed a written test, took a physical, underwent one day of training, and received his taxi license, holding out no hope whatsoever that this job would actually work. From the many movies he had seen about New York City, he assumed that cab drivers spent most of their time racing frantically up and down the streets, scanning the sidewalks and hoping to spot someone who needed a cab. Since his hometown was not as populated as New York City, he was afraid there might not be enough customers to accommodate all the taxicabs in town. On the day he received his license he took a bus to his apartment, and during the ride he began seeing taxis everywhere. It seemed like every other driver on the road was seated inside a Yellow cab, or a Checker cab, or one of the outlaw cabs that prowled the side streets. He couldn't help but conclude that the competition was going to be horrific, and he hated competition. And because he actually liked the idea of having a job that did not involve foremen watching his every move, he also concluded that he wouldn't make one thin dime. On the first day of his new job, after leasing a taxi, he drove out of the Yellow Cab parking lot mumbling, "This is never going to work."

Chapter 36

Jeremy spent that first day transporting businessmen to and from the downtown hotels. Most of his fares tipped well, and at the end of the day he discovered that he had earned fifty dollars in clear profit. He took a bus home that evening in a state of shock. When he got back to his cheap apartment, he emptied all of his pockets and smoothed out the crumpled bills onto his kitchen table. He stared at the pile of money as he ate a plate of canned spaghetti. He was so amazed to have all of this cash that he celebrated by cracking open a second can of spaghetti, something he'd never dared to do before because it might have thrown his budget out of whack. He did not have to perform a great deal of quick mental arithmetic to realize that if he worked for six days in a row he would be able to earn as much money as the government paid him for free in an entire month. What were the political and economic implications of this peculiar truth? He was too tired to think about it, but did anyway. He was surviving on twenty-seven hundred dollars a year from the G.I. Bill, but calculated that if he were to drive a taxi full time instead of going back to school, he could earn more than that in three months. The only thing he ever did in a cab was sit down, and that was the same thing he did in a college classroom. All he ever wanted to be was a writer anyway, not a student, so he figured that if he were to drop out of school, he could be rolling in dough in no time flat. The craving to possess lots of money engulfed Jeremy Bannister that night.

36

Chapter 37

Ironically, Jeremy's natural horror of work won out that summer, and he decided that instead of becoming a full-time taxi driver he would go back to school. He had a hard time believing that his desire to do nothing at all was even greater than his desire to have money, but it was true. The main reason that he wanted to become a big-shot novelist was that novelists did not have to get up and go to work at a laundromat or a warehouse every morning. Novelists could sleep until noon if they so desired. They could loll around in bed all day and gaze at patterns on the ceiling. They could relax on terraces and sip cocktails and watch glorious sunsets. They could hop into Lear jets and fly off to the islands and hobnob with the quaint locals. They could stay up late into the night watching TV, not that Jeremy intended to own a television, for his two years in college had taught him that the very existence of television was rotting the mental fabric of society. It was preventing children from dashing out of doors and taking part in healthy fitness programs. It was even preventing them from reading books. Just the thought of all the things that television programs had done to his own mind made Jeremy pull his taxi over to the curb one afternoon and leap out. He shook his fist at the sky and vowed to never again watch a TV as long as he breathed, regardless of the fact that a Humphrey Bogart film festival was scheduled to start on Channel 2 that same evening. Jeremy Bannister had made his third artistic statement.

Chapter 38

On his last day of driving before returning to school, Jeremy sat in the cab line at the airport wondering if he should fly back to State U just to impress anyone who might be around to notice his arrival. Then he began contemplating the fact that it had been five years since he had graduated from high school. He originally was supposed to have become a big-shot novelist three years ago. Even if he subtracted his two years in the army, he was still one year behind in his schedule. This made him feel a little bit depressed, as well as uneasy. He considered the fact that he had decided when he was ten years old that he wanted to become a big-shot novelist, which meant that he had been trying to become a writer for thirteen years and had not only not written a single word of a novel, he was driving a taxicab for a living. But the potentially depressing irony of these realities was offset by the fact that he had two thousand dollars in the bank. He had never had that much money in his life, not even after his army discharge, when he had one thousand dollars saved up from the war. He had felt rich then, and had mistakenly thought that the money would last him for years. Strangely, there was something about having all this cab money that lessened the sense of urgency that had always driven his desire to become a big-shot novelist. Then Jeremy saw his last fare of the summer season waving to him from the front door of the airport terminal, so he stopped thinking about writing and drove up to the door like a lazy rich man.

Chapter 39

When Jeremy returned to school he again found that all of the apartments were rented. But he yawned with derision, for he had more than two thousand dollars plus G.I. Bill money to tide him over until he could locate a vacant apartment. He rented his old room at the seedy hotel, chuckling at the whimsy of déjà vu, though he was vexed to discover that the rent had risen to seventy-five dollars a week. This forced him to do some quick mental arithmetic while settling in that night. He figured that he could easily live here for nine months, barring tuition, books, food, and other trivial items. He remembered how one year earlier he had successfully survived eating almost nothing but cheese crackers and feasting on one can of spaghetti per day. He felt a certain amount of pride welling up inside him at the idea that he was learning the ropes when it came to suffering and surviving as a writer. The only thing really left to do was start a novel, and he figured he might as well get to work on it. The first thing he did, after he got his clothes put away and his bed made and the floor swept, was put into motion an idea that had been percolating in his mind all summer long. He went to a liquor store and bought a six-pack of beer and drank it, then staggered to the grocery store and bought the latest *Aspiring Writer Magazine*. He grinned goofily at the cashier as she rang up the item. Jeremy had learned from Joe, Jock, and Speed that a determined man could accomplish just about anything if he was drunk enough.

Chapter 40

Jeremy originally had intended to room again with Joe, Jock, and Speed, and had broached the subject at the end of last spring during a particularly riotous hangover. Joe and Jock left the room, leaving Speed to explain that Jeremy would not be living with them during the fall semester. "You drink too much," Speed said. Considering the source of this critique, Jeremy was forced to take it seriously. Not even all of his army buddies combined had ever drunk as much beer as Joe, Jock, and Speed, yet Jeremy outshined them all. Even though Jeremy had never been much of a drinker before going to college, he had come to learn many things about drinking from his roommates, such as tapping a keg, chugging beer, and keeping frosted glasses in the icebox. Jeremy had become so adept at these things that his roommates had declared him the Official Beer Gofer and sent him on beer runs during the middle of keggers when supplies started running low and the guests started complaining. Thanks to all of those goddamn army push-ups he was able to walk a mile to the liquor store and carry back two cases on his shoulders. But Jeremy began wondering if the explanation was merely an excuse that his friends had concocted in order to avoid telling him the real reason they didn't want him back. But they were engineering majors, so he didn't really feel that they possessed the creative imaginations that were necessary to come up with such an ingenious excuse. Thus he was forced to conclude that they were telling the truth.

Chapter 41

That fall Jeremy took an English course in which the works of James Joyce would be studied, not counting *Finnegans Wake*, which the teacher said he was not going to make them read, although he did mention that it took him three years to get through it when he had been an undergraduate and a graduate. Jeremy knew a little about James Joyce, the greatest writer in the world, but had never dared to pick up one of his books. He had always felt that he was not quite ready to approach the master and gaze upon his immortal words. He had seen copies of Joyce's books in the college library but had walked hurriedly past them. Just knowing that he was in the presence of incredible thoughts made him sweaty with excitement. But now he was required to read three of James Joyce's books. Although he breezed through *Dubliners* and *A Portrait of the Artist as a Young Man*, he was not able to breeze through *Ulysses*. Whenever he tried to read it, his mind wandered inexplicably. Sometimes he read it standing up, afraid that if he sat down he would fall asleep. On the day that he finally finished reading Ulysses, he fell asleep. After waking up, he walked over to the campus and wandered around in front of the student union building, having what he took to be an epiphany. He finally knew what kind of a writer he wanted to be. He wanted to be an artist writer. He dashed back to his seedy hotel room, lit a candle, and burned every short story and epic poem that he had ever written. Then he heard a knock on his door.

Chapter 42

"No cooking in the rooms," said the desk clerk, an old man who stood on his tiptoes and craned his neck to get a peek inside. Jeremy blocked the doorway and swallowed hard. "I'm not cooking anything," he said. The desk clerk gave him the fish-eye. Jeremy then realized that if he was going to devote the rest of his life to being a great artist, he would have to embrace The Truth at all times. "I'm burning sheets of typing paper," he said, but before he could elaborate further on the nature of the sheets, the desk clerk told him to be out of there by noon the next day. The next day it began snowing. Jeremy packed his suitcases, checked out of the seedy hotel, and trudged toward the college campus. When he got there, the campus appeared deserted. He was the only person in the snow. The sidewalks were buried under drifts, so Jeremy wasn't certain whether he was walking on the sidewalk or on a pond that he knew was somewhere around there. It was the worst blizzard of the quarter. He made his way in the general direction of the student union building, which was like a large dark shadow in the distance. It was the only place he could think of that he could wait inside without arousing suspicion. He needed a warm place where he could think about what he was going to do next. He didn't think he could walk and think at the same time. As he plowed across the snow-covered grass in front of the student union building, three words kept running through his mind: "art," "truth," and "suffering."

Chapter 43

The student union looked to be deserted too, although Jeremy did hear the occasional distant scrape of shoes belonging to the students involved in the work/study programs. He wandered into a long hallway that was lined with benches. He set his suitcases down and sat on one of the benches in a frigid daze, staring at a puddle of water forming around his tennis shoes. His head was frozen, but he tried to calculate how much money he still had left in the bank. The closest he could come to was four hundred dollars. This served to calm as well as panic him simultaneously. Where did all his money go? His plan to live all year at the hotel had proven to be unrealistic. There had been so much money that he didn't pay any attention when he went out to buy spaghetti. He recalled his carefree taxi days of summer when he was making fifty bucks per shift hand over fist—and back then he had a place to live. He decided that the first thing he ought to do was go find a phone book and look up a few seedy hotels. But then he started wondering if that desk clerk might already have blackballed him with all the other desk clerks in town. The Word might be out. Then he wondered if he could somehow secretly live inside the student union like some sort of mysterious phantomlike wraith. Or perhaps his parents would let him come back home if he agreed to pay them four hundred dollars in advance. As he was mulling these possibilities over, he noticed a sign across the hall that said, "Student Housing Office."

Chapter 44

For some reason, Jeremy had never known that there was a student housing office. It certainly sounded like the sort of place that might be able to help. Afraid that his suitcases would get stolen if he left them in the hallway, which he wanted to do, Jeremy lugged them into the office and set them down, trying with a bit of difficulty to control his facial expression, aware that anyone entering this office carrying suitcases would probably look rather foolish. Jeremy hoped he merely looked desperate, which might not be as bad. A young man was lounging behind a desk. He had long hair and a mustache, and looked cool. "How may I help you?" he said. Jeremy started to describe the process by which he had lost his hotel room, but then he just said he needed an apartment. The man sat up and opened a desk drawer and pulled out a manila folder. "This is a good time of year to be looking for a new place," he said as he set the folder on the desk. "All of the dropouts have left plenty of vacancies." He opened the folder and spun it around so Jeremy could check out the contents. "This is our current listing of available places in town. It's mostly kids looking for roommates. It's pretty hard to find an apartment that's completely vacant right at this time of year. The kinds of students who live alone in apartments are fairly mature and serious about their studies. A lot of them are war veterans who don't want to be interrupted by wild parties." Jeremy started to say something, then remained silent and looked the list over.

Chapter 45

Jeremy pretended to be checking the list carefully, but he was really just taking as long as possible because his head was still frozen. So were his hands because he didn't own any gloves. He didn't own a hat either, since hats weren't "in" these days. As he stared at the list he saw a vacancy that went for ninety dollars per month. The advisor told him that the listing had been posted by a graduate student in economics named Fontaine, who was looking for a roommate. Jeremy said he might want to check that out, so the man made a quick phone call for him, then wrote the address on a slip of paper. Jeremy left the building carrying his suitcases and trudged through the snow toward the address in his pocket. The snow was no longer falling, but there were three-foot drifts on the sidewalks. The apartment he was seeking was located one block off the campus, which was a relief to Jeremy, since his former hotel room had been two miles off the campus and the only footgear he owned were tennis shoes. It now occurred to him that it was a good thing that he had burned all of his fiction manuscripts that had the pseudonym "Fontaine" typed on them. He was in no mood to hear any more pointed questions. When he arrived at the address, he was amazed, for it was a three-story mansion that looked like it was owned by a millionaire. He checked the slip of paper again and realized that the address, 1498 East Main, was followed by a numeral: 1/2. It was the address of a small house, barely a shanty, at the back of the big house.

Chapter 46

Fontaine turned out to be a rather tall, skinny, crew-cut student who was wearing thick glasses. He opened the shanty door and stood studying his new roommate curiously, as if Jeremy were a blackboard. After a moment Fontaine smirked and said, "Come on in." He held the door open for Jeremy, who hurried inside. "Jesus, don't you own a hat?" Fontaine said as Jeremy shook the snow from his head. "I lost it," Jeremy lied. "Where's your gloves?" Fontaine said, and Jeremy told him that someone had stolen them when he was at the student center. "You'll have your own bedroom here," Fontaine said, shutting the door. "This place used to be the servant quarters for the rich bastards who lived in the mansion." Jeremy was surprised at how large the inside of the shanty was. It had looked so small from outside. In the army he had found this to be true of tents. "Who lives in the mansion now?" he said, setting his suitcases down on the living room floor. Fontaine flopped down on an overstuffed chair. "The rich bastard grandchildren, I guess," he said. He looked Jeremy up and down and said, "What's your major?" Jeremy began taking off his coat, trying not to get snow on the floor. "English," he said, and in order to reassure his new roommate that he had not invited a loser into his shanty, he quickly added, "but my long-range goal in life is to someday become a big-shot novelist." Fontaine sat slouched in his chair staring at Jeremy for a few moments, then he said, "You have got to be fucking kidding me."

Chapter 47

Jeremy quickly asked where he might hang up his coat, and Fontaine pointed at an open doorway. "Your room is through there." Fontaine told him that the rent would be ninety dollars a month each. As Jeremy walked into his room he hollered back that this would be satisfactory. Fontaine got up and followed him into the room. "If you want to bring girls in here, it's all right," he said. "Just introduce them to me first. I like to know who the hell's in my house." Jeremy nodded. He didn't even know any girls on a personal basis. He noted that the bedroom was bigger than his old hotel room. Those servants certainly had lived like kings. He went and got his suitcases and began unpacking. He didn't have much to unpack, but since Fontaine was standing in the doorway watching him, he began pretending to sort through his socks. Fontaine started to walk into the living room, then he turned back and said, "You don't smoke, do you, Bannister?" Jeremy quickly shook his head no. "You don't have to worry about that. I've never smoked." Fontaine frowned and said, "Too bad. I'm out of cigarettes. I guess I'll have to hike to the goddamned store. By some miracle you don't happen to own a car do you?" Jeremy told him no. Fontaine shook his head with what appeared to be exasperation. He went into the living room and put on his hat, coat, and gloves and headed for the front door. Just before he stepped outside he glanced at Jeremy, laughed an enigmatic laugh, and said, "You remind me of Dawson." Then he was gone.

47

Chapter 48

Jeremy quickly put away his socks and other clothes, embarrassed to not own very much of anything. Once he became a millionaire writer he intended to own a lot of things, like the mansion out front. When Fontaine got back from the store he sat down on the overstuffed chair and turned on the TV. Jeremy stayed in his room as long as he could stay without making Fontaine think he was hiding, then he stepped out into the living room. Fontaine turned the sound down on the TV and suggested that they have a talk to get to know each other. Jeremy sat down on a chair and tried very hard not to look at *Bewitched*. Even though Fontaine knew Jeremy didn't smoke, he offered him a cigarette anyway. Jeremy waved it off. "I thought all of you writers smoked," Fontaine said. "I'm not published," Jeremy admitted. Fontaine then started asking pointed questions. "You were in the goddamned war?" he exclaimed. "Yes, I served in the infantry." "On whose side?" Fontaine said. "Why . . . on our side," Jeremy replied. Fontaine squinted at him. "Did you ever kill anybody?" Jeremy thought about this for a moment, then said, "No." Fontaine gazed at the smoldering tip of his cigarette. "So you plan to be a novelist, huh?" Jeremy shifted uncomfortably on his chair and said, "That's my basic plan." Fontaine blew out a stream of smoke and said, "Do you know what the combined average annual income of all novelists is?" Jeremy shook his head no. "It's zero," Fontaine said, "minus a few irrelevant decimal points."

Chapter 49

Jeremy did his best to avoid Fontaine after that first night in the shanty. He threw himself into his studies and kept his door shut tight because he didn't want Fontaine to hear the sound of his typewriter clicking. He stayed in his room all the time, not counting going to the bathroom. He and Fontaine took the final tests for the fall quarter prior to the Christmas break, and on the day after finals were over Fontaine knocked on Jeremy's door and asked if he could read some of his writing. Jeremy was flabbergasted, since nobody had ever asked to read any of his prose before. Now he regretted that he had burned everything he'd written. "I don't have anything new to show you right at the moment," he replied with a sense of mournfulness. Fontaine smirked. "I'm going back to my goddamned home over the Christmas break. Why don't you put something together for me to read when I get back?" After Fontaine left, Jeremy spent two weeks trying to rewrite some of the stuff he had burned, wracking his brain to remember any of it. He finally gave up and decided to write a short story in the James Joyce vein. He was delighted to find that the words came easily, now that he was no longer burdened by the concept of "plot." When Fontaine got back, Jeremy handed him the story. Fontaine took it into his room to read while Jeremy sat waiting with trepidation in the living room. Fontaine eventually stormed out of his room, shook the short story in front of Jeremy's startled eyes, and barked, "What the hell is this shit?"

49

Chapter 50

After Fontaine calmed down, Jeremy explained that his story had been inspired by James Joyce's *Ulysses*. He asked if Fontaine had read *Ulysses*, and Fontaine replied, "Not on your fucking life." Jeremy explained that it was a novel about an Irishman walking around Dublin. "What else does the bastard do?" Fontaine said. "He thinks great thoughts, but it's really James Joyce thinking great thoughts," Jeremy said. He told him that the incomprehensible style of his story was referred to as "experimental" by the literary critics. Fontaine lit a cigarette and flopped down on his chair. He leaned forward with his elbows on his knees and frowned. "Let me get this straight," he said. "Are you saying you actually like James Joyce, for godsake?" Jeremy cleared his throat and replied, "Yes I do as a matter of fact." He shifted uncomfortably on his chair, then smiled and said, "I suppose that when it comes to great literature, I'm sort of a snob." Fontaine smirked at him, then leaned back in his chair, took a long pull on his cigarette, and exhaled. "Nah, you're not a snob, Bannister. A snob is a successful bastard who lords it over everybody else. I would say that you fall into the category of a phony." Jeremy was truly shocked by this statement. He had never met anyone so blatantly honest in his life. Something must have shown on Jeremy's face, because Fontaine then said, "Don't take it too hard, but a phony is someone who acts like a successful bastard but isn't. You've got a long way to go before you'll qualify as a snob."

Chapter 51

Even though he tried, Jeremy found it very difficult to avoid Fontaine, since their shanty wasn't all that big to begin with. He wished he were still living in his former landlady's house where he could sneak in and out the back without being seen. Fontaine made him a bit edgy about his ambitions in life. Whenever he wrote theme papers he typed normally, but when he wrote fiction he self-consciously pressed softly on the typewriter keys so Fontaine wouldn't hear the sounds and suspect what he was up to. Unfortunately, this caused the ink to be barely legible on the pages. If Fontaine was at a class, Jeremy would type as fast as possible, but all of the words would be misspelled. He finally decided that he would type his short stories out loud, and if Fontaine asked him what he was doing, he would say he was writing a theme paper, although Fontaine never asked him anything. One night Jeremy got drunk on beer and made his monthly pilgrimage to the supermarket and bought a copy of *Aspiring Writer Magazine*. When he got back to the shanty he discovered Fontaine seated in the living room in a bathrobe, smoking a cigarette and watching *Branded*. "What the hell is that?" Fontaine said, pointing at the magazine, which Jeremy had dropped while stumbling through the doorway. Fontaine got up and crossed the room, snatched the magazine off the floor, and peered at the title. Jeremy waited for his trademark smirk, but Fontaine merely browsed through the magazine, then handed it back and said, "You're gonna need this."

51

Chapter 52

As a result of his year of living drunk with Joe, Jock, and Speed, Jeremy had become somewhat sensitive to the idea of keeping his living quarters neat and tidy. Prior to that he had never really been very concerned about the cleanliness of his apartments, but he had never drunk alone either. Although he now made it a practice to get drunk at least once a month, he was very conscientious about cleaning up anything he soiled or ruined during magazine night. He would crawl out of his bed the next afternoon and prowl about the shanty looking for spilled beer, or crushed cans, or paper airplanes, or anything else that might turn up after his scheduled debauch. Often the things he found surprised him, such as a birdbath. While Fontaine was an acceptably fastidious student, he did not seem overly concerned about the hygienic state of the shanty, barring any unidentifiable liquids on the floor. On the day after his very first magazine night in the shanty, Jeremy had gotten a plastic trash bag from the kitchen and began prowling about the living room gathering up garbage while Fontaine sat smoking and watching *Mannix*. Jeremy tried hard not to make any noise, and whenever he had to cross in front of the television, he dashed. Fontaine put up with this for a while, then said, "Why are you so goddamn obsessed with cleaning everything?" Jeremy frowned at him and replied, "I happen to believe that being neat and tidy is very important." Fontaine smirked and said, "Who told you that, your dead mother?"

52

During the winter quarter of Jeremy's junior year in college he decided that the time had come to sign up for a creative-writing class. He knew that sooner or later he would have to hand in stories that would be discussed in a classroom situation, so he felt he might as well start getting it over with now. Aside from Fontaine, nobody except editors had ever read a single word of his prose fiction. He had often tried to talk people into reading his stories, but they were always too busy, or else just said no. He was a bit intimidated by the idea of eventually showing his work to college seniors, for surely they had to be as talented as anybody who lived in New York City. But he was willing to put up with any derision they might offer him in exchange for the vast knowledge that he would gain from their insightful critiques. During registration he signed up for Creative Writing 301. On the first day of class the teacher informed the students that every short story had a beginning, a middle, and an end. It also had a plot, characters, and a setting, as well as rising and falling action, and some kind of conflict. He said that conventional short stories also had a denouement, in case the students happened to be interested in that sort of writing. The teacher had once been published in a literary magazine, so he told them to buy a copy of an anthology in which his story had been reprinted. It would serve as their textbook. He then told them that their first short story was to be handed in next week, and he dismissed the class.

Chapter 54

Dazzled by his first creative-writing class, Jeremy rushed back to his shanty and got out his dictionary. He was eager to find out exactly what a denouement was. When he found out, he closed the dictionary with delight. It was French! He had no idea how he was going to juggle the vast amounts of information that the teacher had imparted to the class. Rising and falling action! Character! Setting! Good lord, would he be able to weave all of these concepts together into a single coherent narrative? And what about the next class, and the next, and all the classes to come? He would have to buy a giant notebook to contain all of the information that he was destined to be taught. Jeremy went to the student bookstore and bought a new typewriter ribbon, a big bottle of Wite-Out, a box of Number 2 pencils, and a giant notebook. When he got in line at the cash register he tried to control his facial expression so the other students wouldn't know what he was up to. After he got home he thought about trying to rewrite some of his old short stories again, but then decided that since this was the dawn of a new era, he ought to write something new. Using the hot tips that he had received in class, he sat down and began composing a short story. Because he was still enamored of James Joyce's style, he chose to go with an experimental approach in order to impress the seniors in the class. That night he pulled out all the stops and wrote a short story that consisted of a single sentence thirty-five hundred words long.

Chapter 55

One week later Jeremy trudged silently home from his creative-writing class in somewhat of a state of shock. He had handed in xeroxed copies of his story, which had been read by every student in the class, and when it came time to discuss the story, something not unlike a riot had erupted in the room. The teacher had been forced to tell the seniors to stop tossing derision at Jeremy. When he got back to the shanty he found Fontaine slouched in his chair, smoking a cigarette, and watching *That Girl*. Fontaine had agreed to read Jeremy's short story the previous night but had not made a single comment on it, other than to hand it back to Jeremy with an enigmatic blank face. "How did the sentence go over?" he said as soon as Jeremy walked in. Jeremy looked at him with something not unlike horror in his eyes. "Not so good," he replied. Fontaine blew out a long stream of smoke and said, "Tore it to shreds, huh?" Jeremy nodded. Fontaine smirked. He sat up straight in his chair and said, "Can I assume that you will be discussing the short stories of all the other students in your class during the weeks to come?" Jeremy nodded and sat down heavily on the chair that he sat on when he was not hiding in his room. "In that case," Fontaine went on, "I would like to know if you've ever read a book titled *The Prince* by Machiavelli." "No," Jeremy said. Fontaine nodded and said, "Allow me to sum up Machiavelli's basic philosophy in one succinct sentence: right now every student in that class is scared shitless of you."

Chapter 56

Although Fontaine was only a student of economics, he seemed to know a great deal about human nature. Jeremy had never asked him exactly what economics was about, but he assumed it involved cold-blooded numbers, as well as money, statistics, computers, and other stuff that had nothing to do with the sad plight of humanity. So he was a bit surprised when Fontaine began explaining that it was human nature for writers to savagely attack a defenseless story like a pack of wolves devouring a downed cow. Jeremy took this to mean that his story was defenseless, but he was too depressed to make up any phony excuses. "The next time your class meets, the smell of blood will be in the air," Fontaine said. He seemed to be talking to himself as he gazed at a curl of cigarette smoke rising toward the ceiling. "Your job will be to seek out the tiniest of flaws in their stories and build them into mammoth literary blunders. Take no prisoners and show no mercy, that's the only way to handle those bastards." Jeremy nodded thoughtfully. "I suppose I could try that. I've been told that revenge is sweet." Fontaine blew a smoke ring and watched it dissipate. "Sugar is shit compared to revenge," he said. After Jeremy returned from his next creative-writing class, he told Fontaine that he just couldn't bring himself to say anything bad about the student story that had been discussed in class because it was just too well written. Fontaine gave him the fish-eye and said, "How the hell would you know?"

Chapter 57

When Jeremy originally moved in with Fontaine he thought he would at last be able to get started on a novel. He had found it somewhat difficult to work on prose fiction when he had lived in the seedy hotel, due to screams and thuds that erupted at odd hours of the day. But by the time spring break rolled around he hadn't written a single novel. He'd spent all his time writing either theme papers for his English classes or short stories that never impressed the seniors in the creative-writing class that he had come to dread. At some point he began to get the feeling that his writing career was going nowhere, and that college was just a waste of time. He didn't seem to be learning anything about how to write novels. Thus, he made a fateful decision: "I can't live here anymore." On the evening of the last day of classes he got drunk in his room, then walked into the living room where Fontaine was chain-smoking and watching *The Flying Nun*. Jeremy announced that he would not be returning to school following spring break. Fontaine looked up at him. "You remind me exactly of Dawson," he said. Jeremy was about to ask who Dawson was, but then decided he probably didn't want to know. Fontaine sat up in the chair and peered at Jeremy. "So what are you going to do with your life?" he said. Jeremy shrugged. "Go back home and drive a taxicab and write novels." Fontaine smiled kindly and said, "Listen, Bannister. Take my advice. Forget James Joyce. Crank out some commercial garbage. That's where the real money is."

Chapter 58

Jeremy Bannister was twenty-three years old when he dropped out of his junior year of college, but he was still leery about telling his parents. He could never quite forget the night his father had railed at him after he had made his first artistic statement. In fact, his father had never actually ceased railing about that almost-touchdown right up to the day he told his son to leave home. So Jeremy decided not to tell his parents about his almost-college degree. He would just start living his life and let his parents find out about it by accident, if they ever found out at all. On the day he arrived at the bus station in his hometown, he took a Yellow cab to Yellow Cab and signed up for another tour of duty. This was how he thought of cab driving. It was just like going back into the army, minus the push-ups. He rented a cheap apartment and unpacked his suitcases, and reminded himself not to purchase a TV. After he got all his worldly belongings put away he walked over to a nearby drugstore and bought a new typewriter ribbon, a big bottle of Wite-Out, a box of Number 2 pencils, and a giant notebook. But due to his apprehension about having made such a radical move in his literary career as dropping out of college, he couldn't write that night. On his first day back on the job, he drove his cab to a hotel and got into the line. As he was waiting for a fare, he did some quick mental arithmetic and calculated that when June and his birthday arrived he would be four years behind his original schedule to become a big-shot novelist.

Chapter 59

Now that he lived in an apartment building where he never saw his neighbors and was required to mail his rent check every month because the owner was an absentee landlord, Jeremy was at last able to put into motion a three-year-long dream. He sent away for a one-year subscription to *Aspiring Writer Magazine*, hoping that he would need it for only one year. He had wanted to do this when he lived with Fontaine, but he had felt edgy about the idea that Fontaine would see the magazine in the mail once a month and would say stuff. Except for the one issue that Fontaine had seen, Jeremy had been able to sneak the magazines into the shanty by hiding them up a coat sleeve. It warmed his heart when the very first subscription issue arrived in brown paper. Nobody would ever know his secret, except the mailman. Jeremy ripped open the issue and spent the evening gorging himself on hot tips. Just reading this magazine made him feel like he was an integral part of the literary world. He even took the magazine with him when he drove his taxi. One day he was sitting in the cab line at the airport perusing an article about agents and wondering if he ought to go ahead and get one, when a cab driver walked past his window and said, "*Aspiring Writer Magazine*, huh? I got me a shitload of old issues if you want to borrow them." Rattled, Jeremy quickly closed the magazine and told the man that one of his fares had left it in the backseat. The driver smirked at him and said, "Yeah, the fares leave them in the backseats of all our cabs."

Chapter 60

To Jeremy's annoyance, the driver who had offered him a shitload of magazines began hanging around whenever Jeremy showed up to work the airport. His name was Bud, and he liked to talk a lot. "A guy down the line has a portable TV in his cab," Bud said. "That's illegal." Bud seemed to know an awful lot about things people shouldn't do. It seemed like every person he gossiped about was either doing something illegal or was treading on thin ice. Jeremy tried to avoid Bud whenever he could, and would have stayed away from the airport altogether, except working the airport was easier than using the radio to pick up fares—that way the radio dispatcher wasn't yelling at him all the time. Jeremy wanted cab driving to be as easy as possible. Much to Jeremy's consternation, one day Bud asked, "Have you ever gotten published?" It seemed apparent that Bud had seen right through his feeble ruse. "Not really," Jeremy replied. Bud nodded like a man in the know. "You ought to talk to some of these other drivers," he said. "They're just like you." Jeremy wasn't quite able to follow the logic there, and he wished the goddamn cab line would start moving. "You should go to The Cork Room some night," Bud said in a confidential tone of voice. "That's where all of us cab novelists hang out." Jeremy's interest was somewhat piqued by this advice. "What's The Cork Room?" he said. "It's a bar," Bud said. "Even writers who don't drive taxis go there. The joint sells wine by the shot. That's illegal, but the fix is in."

60

Chapter 61

Jeremy was leery about going to a bar where writers hung out, especially writers who didn't drive cabs. Writers like that probably were published. He had always been interested in talking to other people who were trying to be novelists, but he didn't want to be condescended to by published writers. Of course, he had written quite a number of short stories, as well as one epic poem, so he figured he could hold his own against condescending bastards. But sooner or later they would probably ask pointed questions about his publishing history, and he would have to admit that he was perhaps not actually qualified to claim the title of "Writer" yet. This was the fly in the ointment of his literary career. He thought maybe he should wait until he had published at least one short story before he stepped into a den of novelists, otherwise it would be like going to war without any ammo. But he decided to take a chance and visit the bar to see what it was all about. One morning while driving to the airport he made a detour past The Cork Room to get the layout. He wanted to know exactly what he was getting into. It was a small innocuous bar on the main drag, too far away from his apartment to walk to at night. He would probably have to take a bus. A few taxis were parked in the adjacent lot, which Jeremy found odd, since you were not allowed to drink and drive in a taxicab. In fact, it was illegal. As he drove toward the airport, Jeremy suddenly began to worry that he was turning into another Bud.

Chapter 62

On the night that Jeremy took the big step and went to The Cork Room, he discovered that the taxi drivers who parked their cabs in the adjacent lot were not drinking alcohol. They were nursing soda pops and chauffeuring back and forth the writers who didn't drive cabs. The Cork Room was a cash cow to drivers in the know. Jeremy decided to take a city bus to the bar that Saturday night. He would have taken a cab but he felt that cabs were too expensive, and he was afraid the driver might take him on the scenic route. Jeremy himself had never taken a fare on the scenic route because he was afraid he would get lost, and ultimately would get caught. He stood outside the bar and listened for the raucous sounds of laughter and music, assuming that a drinking establishment full of writers would sound like a college dorm. But he heard no raucous sounds. He went on inside and pretended to use the pay phone, calling his own apartment and casually glancing around the room to get the layout. It was easy to spot the cab drivers, with their blue jeans and yellow caps. The non-drivers were easy to spot too because they were wearing tweed jackets and were smoking pipes. Classical music was playing softly over a loudspeaker. He didn't see a jukebox. He was already starting to love this joint. He hung up the phone and went to the bar and ordered his first shot of red wine ever. At that point Bud walked in the front door and spotted him. "Hey pal, you finally made it!" he shouted. "Hey everybody, this is a new writer!"

Chapter 63

Jeremy bristled inwardly at this abrupt introduction to his new milieu. He preferred to take things slowly in life, easing into new situations by testing the waters and not leaping blindly, which he suspected explained why he was four years behind schedule as a big-shot novelist. He felt foolish being introduced as a writer, since he had never been published and had never managed to get started on writing an actual novel. Bud began calling out to familiar cronies seated at tables around the room. As he did so, Jeremy turned on his barstool and began nodding in the general direction of the men who were waving back. He tried very hard to control his facial expression. He didn't want anyone to think that he had come in here to lord it over them, while at the same time he did not want to make himself look so humble that someone might lord something over on him. But since Bud was the first person in the world who had ever described him as a "Writer," a modest and uncontrollable smile of humility formed on Jeremy's lips, as though he was conceding the possibility that he might deserve this grandiose title. His nods of greeting were met by dark glares and the rapid puffing of pipes, which made the ashes glow like small campfires. "This guy drives a taxi for Yellow Cab!" Bud explained. The bills of a few caps here and there moved up and down as if in greeting. Then Jeremy's worst nightmare came true. From a dimly lit corner of the bar someone hollered, "Has he ever been published?"

Chapter 64

Jeremy's first night in The Cork Room was to remain somewhat of an indistinct blur in his memory banks. He had never drunk any sort of wine before, and had learned that traditionally it wasn't supposed to be chugged. When he woke up the next afternoon in his apartment, certain events drifted in and out of his mind like the disjointed previews of an avant-garde European film. He clearly recalled Bud escorting him over to a table and introducing him to various writers, some of them cabbies and some of them just regular people. Bud explained that Jeremy had never been published anywhere before, although he was a reader of *Aspiring Writer Magazine*, "Which makes him one of us!" The writers at the table had appeared rather satisfied by the news that Jeremy had not yet been published. They seemed to take an especial liking to him after that. They began asking him how many rejection slips he had collected, and whether he had a literary agent, or if he knew how to get an agent. They were also curious to learn if he had ever completed the first draft of a novel. It seemed to lift their spirits even higher when he said no, and they began buying him shots of red wine. Jeremy admitted up front that he had ambitions to be a published novelist someday, but it wasn't until much later in the evening that he started using the phrase "big-shot novelist." Now he wished he hadn't said that. What if all of the writers in The Cork Room began referring to him as "The Big-Shit Novelist" behind his back?

Chapter 65

Even though he seemed to remember having a good time in The Cork Room, Jeremy finally couldn't bring himself to return to the bar. He had absolutely no idea what events had taken place after the last ones he could remember, but some intuitive sense told him that they were awful. While he had no specific reason to feel embarrassed, he nevertheless felt embarrassed anyway. This used to happen to him with frequency when he lived with Joe, Jock, and Speed, but he was able to overcome it back then simply by getting drunk again. However, he had to go to work every day now, so that strategy was down the crapper. Whenever he drove his taxi he stayed away from the airport cab line where he might run into Bud. He was a bit shaken up by the sheer weirdness of not being able to remember almost any of the things that had taken place that night in the bar. He couldn't remember any time in his life when he couldn't remember anything. He did have a vague memory of Bud driving him home, but it was all too much to dwell upon. From now on he just wanted to remain in his apartment at night and avoid people. As a consequence, Jeremy finally got around to starting his first novel. There wasn't anything else to do at night since he didn't own a TV. He sat down at his typewriter one evening and began cracking his knuckles and fidgeting. He recalled the advice of his college creative-writing teacher to "write what you know about." So he began typing a novel about an English major tormented by an economics graduate.

65

Chapter 66

Jeremy was ecstatic that he had at last started down that long hard road to becoming a novelist. It had taken years to get going, but now he was on his way. On top of buckling down to writing, he also decided that he would wean himself from using the phrase "big-shot novelist" so that he wouldn't accidentally use it again in any bars. Even though he wouldn't be going back to The Cork Room, he assumed that he would one day find himself in other bars where other writers hung out. Writers seemed to like bars. Norman Mailer often went to bars, according to the tabloids—although if through some fluke Jeremy was in a bar with a writer that famous, he expected he wouldn't have the guts to "talk shop." He also expected that it would be difficult to stop saying "big-shot novelist." It seemed like he'd been saying it all his life. Giving it up would probably be as hard as giving up smoking was for smokers. He had come very close to taking up smoking when he had lived with Fontaine. He liked the smell of cigarette smoke. It reminded him of "art" and "truth." He had even toyed a number of times with the idea of buying a pipe, since the dust jackets of many novels had pipe smokers on them. But the odor of pipe smoke reminded him of The Cork Room. Just the memory of that night made him a bit edgy, so he stopped thinking about smoking and concentrated on writing Chapter 1 of his first novel. He finished it in three days. The only problem was, he didn't seem to have any ideas for Chapter 2.

Chapter 67

Jeremy tried to solve the problem of writing Chapter 2 by leafing through a few back issues of *Aspiring Writer Magazine,* looking for an article on how to get an agent. Every other issue seemed to give out hot tips for writers seeking literary agents. One of the brutal truths about the publishing world that he had run across was that it was almost impossible to get a publisher to look at a manuscript "across the transom" since publishers had abandoned the "slush pile" years ago. Sooner or later he would need an agent for that, but he also felt that if he had an agent it would give him the motivation to get on with Chapter 2. Just the knowledge that a literary agent was impatiently waiting for him to finish a novel might have the same effect on him that impatient people always did. He remembered how back in college the prospect of a looming deadline on a theme paper had motivated him to type drunk. He finally found an article that advised writers to send a sample chapter of a novel to an agent along with a detailed outline of the plot. This was just what he was looking for! It was somewhat of a lucky break too, because he already had a sample chapter. All he needed to do now was wrack his brain for some kind of a plot, and he would be on his way. Jeremy strode to his desk and planted himself in front of his typewriter. He rolled a sheet of paper through the platen, cracked his knuckles and fidgeted, and then, calling upon all of the powers of his creative imagination, he began making up a plot.

Chapter 68

The next day Jeremy drove his taxi to a Kwickie-Print and had fifteen copies made of his sample chapter and outline. There seemed to be a lot of people doing this same thing. He wasn't entirely certain, but he thought he recognized one of the customers who was having copies made of an entire manuscript. The man was wearing a tweed jacket, sported a short beard, held an unlit pipe between his teeth, and seemed to be acting rather furtive. Jeremy's sample chapter was twenty pages long. It cost him a lot of money to get all the copies made, and when he left the shop he looked like he was carrying the manuscript of a novel under his arm. Perhaps some of the other people in the shop thought he was a novelist, maybe even that guy who looked like a novelist. The next day Jeremy mailed all of his sample chapters. Two weeks later he came home from work and found fifteen familiar SASEs stuffed into his mailbox. He hurriedly took them up to his apartment and opened them one by one until he had a stack of fifteen rejection slips on his kitchen table. Nobody wanted to look at his novel. Jeremy decided that this was probably a good thing because he had lived for two weeks with the sweaty fear that all of the agents would ask to see his book, and he didn't have one. For two weeks he had felt the same as he had felt in college when his landlady had asked him to rake the leaves. He went into his living room and collapsed onto his couch, relieved that the horror of waiting for acceptance slips was over.

Chapter 69

As he drove his cab the next day Jeremy thought that perhaps it might be best to make a chapter-by-chapter outline of his college novel. Maybe the plot would jell if he knew more of the actual details. But he wasn't entirely certain he could fill up three hundred pages about a tormented student. That same day he picked up a fare at a hotel and drove him to the airport. As he was removing the suitcases he heard a horn honk. He turned around and saw Bud pulling in. Bud hopped out and waved at him, and hollered, "Hey Bannister! Where ya been hiding? Ain't seen ya in a long while!" Jeremy quickly set the suitcases on the sidewalk and began to act as if he had a pressing engagement and couldn't stop to chat, but Bud trapped him near his left rear fender. "The guys down at The Cork Room have been asking about you," he said. Jeremy glanced at his wristwatch with irritation. "They all said they wanted to see you again. You were a real laugh riot that night!" Jeremy stopped glancing impatiently at his watch and said, "Was I?" Bud clapped him on the shoulder and grinned. "Shit yeah," he said. "You had everybody rolling on the floor with all your hilarious college stories." Jeremy smiled, and told Bud that he had been seriously thinking about dropping by again some night but had been just too busy working on a brand-new novel. Bud said he ought to drop in next Saturday night if he was free. Then he said that the two of them should move their taxis. "It's illegal to stand in front of the terminal and talk."

Chapter 70

The following Saturday night Jeremy took a bus to The Cork Room, reminding himself that a shot of red wine was not the equivalent of a shot of beer. As he approached the door, he had the same feeling that he had felt on the night he went with his army buddies to that hooker's apartment after basic training, the sense that he was about to do something ridiculous. As soon as he stepped through the doorway, people began hailing him from the tables. If they had thrown things at him he would not have been surprised, for he was not that certain that Bud had been telling the truth. Jeremy sometimes had the feeling that people were playing tricks on him that he didn't quite get. He had often felt that way when he lived with Joe, Jock, and Speed, especially when they sent him out to lug home cases of beer. Sometimes they would abruptly stop laughing when he trudged back into the apartment. "Getcher keister over here and sit down, Bannister!" hollered a writer wearing a tweed jacket. It may have been the man he had seen at the Kwickie-Print, but he wasn't certain. All of the non-cab writers looked the same. Jeremy sat down, and one of the cab writers asked a waitress to bring him a shot of wine. Jeremy gazed at the faces around the table and realized that he did not recognize a single one of them. "Got any more good stories about that bastard Fontaine?" one of the men said. The group burst out laughing. Jeremy pretended to think this over. "No, I'm pretty certain I told all of my Fontaine stories the last time," he lied.

70

Chapter 71

"Leave it to an economics student to give advice on how to make money," one of the writers said with a sneer. The rest of the writers shook their heads with disgust. Jeremy took a sip of red wine and tried to calculate how much beer it might equal. He intended to drink no more than a six-pack of beer of wine that night. This was a plan that he had devised after the last time he was in here. He had spent a number of nights since then drinking only a six-pack of beer and then wandering around his living room to get a feel for how it felt. If he started to feel that way tonight, he would switch to pop. "So how's your novel coming along?" another writer said. Jeremy started to frown, then quickly controlled his facial expression. How did this man know that he was writing a novel? Did Bud squeal? He hated it when people knew what he was up to. He took a sip of his wine, then made a decision: he could not possibly spend this evening pretending to know what the hell anyone was talking about. "I'm sorry," he said, "but I just don't recall your name." All of the writers burst out laughing, almost as if they had expected such a response. "My name is Hames," the man said. "The last time you were in here you told us that you were working on a new novel exploring the dichotomy of good versus evil." Unable to control his facial muscles, Jeremy frowned, then said, "The truth is, I gave up on that novel." He expected to hear hoots of derision, but he heard no hoots. All of the writers seemed rather pleased that he had given up.

Chapter 72

Jeremy began to feel a little bit foolish talking about his own writing, since he had never gotten any of his short stories published and had completed only one chapter of a novel that had been rejected fifteen times. And he didn't even want to think about the epic poem that he had burned in a fit of artistic inspiration. After his fourth shot of red wine though, Jeremy began to feel excited about talking about his own writing. He told the group that even though he had given up on his last novel, he had already started a new one. Upon hearing this news, a grim expression fell over the face of each man at the table. They began glancing at each other. For the first time in his life, Jeremy felt that he knew exactly what everyone was thinking. The wine began to work on his memory banks, and he recalled a number of things about the first time he was in here. One thing he remembered was that nobody here had ever been published before, except one man, but he couldn't remember who, or even if the guy was seated at the table. "My new novel was inspired by my last visit here, you see," he quickly explained. A few faces ceased to be grim. "Are you putting any of us in it?" a writer said. "No, but after the success of the stories I told you last time, I decided to go ahead and write a novel about my ex-roommate Fontaine." The crowd went completely silent. Then one of the writers said, "Don't waste your time." Jeremy looked at him and said, "Why not?" "Because," another man said, "you have already talked your novel away."

Chapter 73

When Jeremy heard these ominous words, a sweaty fear engulfed him. He had never before heard of the concept of talking a novel away, but it sounded just like something he would do. Even though he hated admitting to anyone that he didn't understand exactly what they were talking about, especially if they were talking about abstract concepts, he asked the writers what they meant. He was worried that his literary career might be at stake. So Hames began explaining the process by which a novel is talked away. "A writer tries to gauge the potential quality of his novel by telling the highlights to both friends and strangers in bars or at parties. If they don't respond favorably, the writer subsequently loses interest in working on his story." Jeremy frowned. "But . . . you guys seemed to enjoy hearing my stories. I thought that they might make an interesting novel." Another writer intervened at this point and said, "When you tell all the good parts of your novel to another person, you lose the spontaneity that you need to write your story. Look it up in the February issue of *Aspiring Writer Magazine*. It's all in there." Jeremy finally began to see the light. "This would probably explain why I can't think up anything to put into chapter two!" he exclaimed. The table erupted with applause, and Hames ordered shots of wine for everyone. When Jeremy rode home in a cab later that evening he felt both exhilarated and relieved, for he no longer had any reason to continue writing his college novel.

Chapter 74

Although Jeremy had never accomplished anything in his lifetime, it seemed to him that giving up on his college novel was a major step toward publication. By abandoning a book that was not worth writing, he was making room for the next book that would one day comprise a part of his body of work. Jeremy felt like he was making progress at last. One afternoon as he was sitting in the cab line, he read an article in the paper that said Damian Greenleaf Bordon would be doing a signing at a local bookstore that night. Jeremy couldn't believe it. Bordon was the most successful novelist in the entire country. Jeremy had bought all nine of his best-selling novels and had read each of them three times, hoping to figure out how Bordon did it. Bordon had been paid five million dollars for each novel, which meant he had forty-five million dollars, not counting the money he used to buy food and houses and cars and other trivial items. Jeremy started to fantasize that he and Bordon might become friends. During the signing Damian Greenleaf Bordon might ask where a decent watering hole was in this town. At that point Jeremy would step forward and recommend The Cork Room. While popping corks, Jeremy would mention that he too dabbled in prose. Bordon would smile with novelist camaraderie, and ask if he might be allowed to read some of his stuff. After Jeremy got off work that day, he put all of his Damian Greenleaf Bordon books into a paper bag and waited patiently for nightfall.

Chapter 75

While Jeremy was standing at the bus stop, the paper bag containing all nine of Bordon's hardback books broke open, so he had to hurry back home and put the novels into a plastic garbage bag. When he arrived at the bookstore, he found a large group of fans waiting to get their Bordon books signed. It was first-come, first-serve, and the owner of the store was handing out tickets to get into line. Jeremy was given ticket number 150. The owner noticed the garbage bag that Jeremy was carrying and told him that Mr. Bordon would be signing only his current novel, which was available for $29.95 at the main desk. Breaking into a sweaty fear, Jeremy hurried to the main desk and bought a copy of *Connecticut Mandate* and got back into line, although he didn't really have to hurry since he was the last person in line. He would have been a bit more embarrassed about holding the garbage bag but for a few other embarrassed-looking people holding paper bags. He then wondered if Bordon would notice the garbage bag and begin asking pointed questions about it. If so, he decided he would tell Bordon that he was a janitor on his way home from his job. He hid the bag behind him and somehow managed to successfully maintain his balance. Damian Greenleaf Bordon was wearing a tweed jacket, had a beard, and looked just like an unpublished writer. After he signed Jeremy's book, Bordon gave him a big smile, stood up from the table and said, "Hey, let's go pop some corks," to a buxom blonde standing next to him.

Chapter 76

Whenever Jeremy visited a bookstore to browse the bestseller shelf, he always felt a bit self-conscious. He suspected that the cashiers suspected him of being an unpublished writer. He suspected most of the male customers of being unpublished writers, especially the men with beards. They stood before the bestseller shelf gazing at the titles as though they were trying to decipher the hidden secret of getting published, just as Jeremy himself was doing. He would saunter up to the shelf and give it a quick look as though he were searching for one particular book and was not all that impressed with what he saw, which he was. How did they do it? How did all of these authors write such thick, successful books? He envisioned the authors seated at desks in their apartments in New York City, hunched over ancient typewriters and smoking pipes and rattling off brilliant prose. Most of them would be tormented by their visions. After putting in eight or ten hours of backbreaking labor battling the blank page, they would flee their garrets and head for tiny bars in Greenwich Village where all the great artists hung out. Jeremy would quickly read the titles on the shelf to see if any new books had arrived since his last visit. He would spend no more than fifteen seconds examining the latest bestsellers before hurrying away, pretending that he had a pressing engagement and hoping that none of the cashiers knew exactly what he had been up to. A quick visit to the bookstore could be sheer hell for Jeremy Bannister.

Chapter 77

Even though it was obvious to Jeremy that any man with a beard was an unpublished writer, he began to think about growing one himself. Many of the writers at The Cork Room had beards, and it made them look somewhat intellectual. He wasn't sure why this was. Possibly it was biblical. Back at State U all of the other male students in his creative-writing class had beards, and they were unpublished writers as far he knew—he couldn't imagine a published writer taking a writing course, unless he was a journalist working on a secret exposé about the evils of higher education. One morning Jeremy got up and performed a rather radical move. He went into the bathroom and stood in front of the mirror and brushed his teeth, but he didn't shave. He went to work with a day's growth of beard on his face feeling more like a bum than a taxi driver. He hoped the dispatcher wouldn't think he was drunk and refuse to give him the key to his taxi. He was also a bit concerned that Bud might see him and know exactly what he was up to. He had come to like Bud, even if the guy was a loudmouth. But that was in Bud's nature. Bud might even make an interesting character to put into an exposé someday about the evils of cab driving. Of course, Jeremy would have to disguise the character in order to avoid getting sued by Bud for one million dollars. According to *Aspiring Writer Magazine,* utilizing friends as characters in a book could sometimes be illegal. Bud could probably fill him in on the details.

Chapter 78

Jeremy decided to avoid working the airport in order to give his beard time to flourish. He didn't want Bud to see him with a half-formed beard. That would be tantamount to showing someone a half-written novel. Jeremy sometimes wondered if he would be able to get a book contract from a publisher by submitting a half-written novel and promising to finish it. Maybe they would give him half of an advance on royalties. But after the sample-chapter disaster, he wasn't sure it would be worth the effort to write two hundred pages just to end up getting another batch of rejection slips. Why bother? He examined his beard every morning and was pleased to note that he was starting to look rather intelligent. Even the bald spot on his left cheek was hidden. The day finally came when Jeremy drove to the airport prepared to face up to Bud's comments, whichever way they might go. He found Bud buying a Twinkie from a snack truck that parked near the cab line every day. He walked up to Bud with a modest smile and waited for his reaction to this bold move in his writing career. Bud did a double take when he saw Jeremy, and quickly said, "That's illegal. You better hope the taxi supervisor doesn't see it." Shocked by this dire warning, Jeremy asked what he was talking about. "Yellow Cab regulations," Bud said. "A beard must be trimmed to half an inch." Baffled, Jeremy looked around at all the other bearded taxi drivers buying snacks. "But they have long beards," he said. Bud nodded. "Wait'll the crackdown."

Chapter 79

While Bud's dire warning that there might someday be a crackdown on beards bothered Jeremy, it didn't cause him to trim his beard short. Bud reminded him of everybody he ever knew in the army. Everybody in the army spread rumors as if doing so was a military regulation, but he had never seen a rumor come true, even though he had always worried about them. He decided he would wait until a rumor came along that said the supervisor was planning to measure beards in the taxi line at the airport the way he sometimes drove up and randomly checked the drivers' turn signals. He considered buying an extra razor and keeping it in the glove compartment of his taxicab. If he ever saw the supervisor firing drivers he might be able to shave off his beard just in time. But the thought of attempting such a desperate ploy made him wonder if looking highly intelligent was really worth it. The following Saturday night he took a bus to The Cork Room. It was time to let his fellow writers both see and pass judgment on his new beard. As soon as he walked in, everybody looked his way. At first they didn't seem to recognize him, so he strolled up to a table where his friends were drinking wine, and said, "Hi guys. It's me, Jeremy Bannister." Hames quickly stood up from the table and grinned, clapping him on the shoulder. "Well, well, well," he said. Hames sported a beard too. "All you need now is a briar pipe and a tweed jacket to round out your image." That was the night Jeremy accidentally set his beard on fire.

Chapter 80

The evening had begun with a series of shots placed in front of Jeremy. The writers congratulated him on this bold literary move with as much enthusiasm as he imagined they would have heaped upon him if he had received an acceptance slip. The only writer here who had ever received an acceptance slip was an elderly man named Rod Lofton. Fifteen years earlier he had published a short story in *Frogblade Magazine*. He was revered by all the other writers. Whenever they had a question about how to get an agent, or how to find an "in" with a publishing company in New York, they would ask Lofton, even though he did not have an agent or anything else. Lofton was the man whom Jeremy had met the first time he had gone to the bar but couldn't remember the second time he had gone there. The only other person he had ever known who had gotten published was his college writing teacher. But Rod Lofton was a "real" person, so Jeremy felt the same sense of awe in his presence that all the other writers felt. Lofton reached into his coat pocket and pulled out a pipe. He handed it to Jeremy and told him of its history. "That's the very same pipe that I was smoking on the night I conceived of 'Barstow,'" which was his only published short story. Jeremy was honored by this gesture. He decided that he would go shopping someday soon and buy a tweed jacket, even though he was a cab driver. He placed the pipe stem between his teeth and felt his IQ beginning to rise. Then someone handed him a match.

Chapter 81

The next morning Jeremy studied the remains of his beard in the mirror and decided that if he trimmed it to half an inch, the damage would not be visible to the naked eye. When he went to work that morning, the dispatcher started to give him the key to his taxi, but then said, "Whoa fella, are you drunk?" Jeremy said no, and pretended that he didn't know what the guy was talking about. As he drove, he kept glancing at his scorched beard in the rearview mirror, wondering if any of his fares were wondering what was wrong with him. Later that afternoon he dropped off a fare at the airport, then drove to the cab line. Bud spotted him and began waving, and shouting, "Hey fireface!" but Jeremy kept on driving as if he had a pressing engagement. He now had acquired two nicknames in his lifetime: "The Big-Shit Novelist" and "Fireface." He didn't know which was worse. He couldn't see himself ever going to The Cork Room again. It was sort of like the first time he had stopped going to The Cork Room, except now he could remember all of the embarrassing things that had taken place. The writers had been forced to pour a carafe of wine on his head. He wished he'd gotten drunk afterwards so the whole mess would be obliterated from his memory banks. He began to get the feeling that he was going to stop being a cab driver. He felt as if his life was about to undergo a major change. As he was mulling this over, it occurred to him that "Fireface" would make a pretty good title for an action-adventure novel.

Chapter 82

Jeremy was amazed that so many ideas could come out of a single title. For the rest of the day he drove his cab and thought about things that could go into a novel called *Fireface*. It could be a horror-suspense genre novel about a mysterious man that everybody called "Fireface." He would commit evil acts, setting things on fire with the flames that erupted from his cheeks and chin. There would be some kind of a plot, as well as rising and falling action, and all the other things that his creative-writing teacher in college had talked about. He might even go so far as to include a denouement. The possibilities were limitless. A book like this might even catch the attention of a movie producer or two—the story could be a real cash cow. But as he thought about the book, a powerful emotion began to wrestle with his soul. How could a young man like himself who was enamored of the works of James Joyce consider lowering himself to writing a blockbuster novel that would make him rich? He was willing to admit that he didn't know a great deal about writing novels, but he did know one thing: a novelist must avoid writing for money at all costs. His teacher back at State U had hammered that truth into his head. Jeremy had gone so far as to write it down in his giant notebook, which had otherwise remained blank. He decided that there was only one thing to do. After he finished driving this evening he would buy a six-pack of beer, go home and get drunk, and spend the rest of the night wrestling with his soul.

Chapter 83

"Good Christ, is that you, Bannister?" Fontaine said at the other end of the phone line. Jeremy was lying on his couch with his phone under his left ear. "Yes it is," he said. "I need your help." There was a pause at the other end of the line. "Are you in jail?" Fontaine said. "No, I'm just at home," Jeremy replied. "Do you have any idea what the hell time it is, for godsake?" Fontaine snarled. "No." "It's three in the goddamned morning!" Jeremy nodded. "I am aware of that," he said, "but I have arrived at an important turning point in my literary career and I need advice." There was another pause, then Fontaine said, "In other words, you're drunk." Jeremy nodded and said, "I am aware of that." He made a move to sit up, but as he did so beer cans cascaded off his body and crashed onto the floor. "What in the hell was that noise?" Fontaine said. Jeremy fell back onto the couch and said, "What noise?" "Jesus H. Christ, you remind me exactly of Dawson," Fontaine grumbled. "What the hell kind of help do you need anyway?" Jeremy explained that he had come up with the plot of a novel that would have absolutely no literary or artistic merit whatsoever, and he was trying to decide whether or not it would be morally reprehensible to become a millionaire off of his artistic gifts. "You don't want advice," Fontaine smirked. "You want permission." Jeremy nodded, and lay waiting for permission. "Go ahead and write the goddamned thing, and while you're at it, don't ever call me back again," Fontaine said, ringing off.

Chapter 84

When Jeremy woke up the next afternoon, he felt a strange sense of elation. He knew that at some point during his wrestling match with his soul he had come to the conclusion that it would be acceptable to write a crass commercial novel, although he could not trace the thread of logic that had led up to his decision. He did not remember his phone call to Fontaine at three o'clock in the morning. He would never remember it as long as he lived. Nevertheless, the decision had been made and he was eager to get going. He began preparing himself mentally and emotionally for the backbreaking labors ahead of him. He was absolutely determined to follow through on the writing of this book, although just the thought of seeing something through to the very end sent a chill down his spine because he couldn't recall ever having done a thing like that before, unless he counted his year in the war, although back then it was like the war was seeing him through to the end. At any rate, he reminded himself never to tell anyone about his new book for fear of talking his novel away, as he'd done with his college novel. The first thing he did the day after his hangover was go to a store and buy a typewriter ribbon, a big bottle of Wite-Out, a box of Number 2 pencils, and a giant notebook. He walked back to his apartment and immediately dusted it top to bottom. He did not want to encounter any distractions after he got going on his new novel. Just before he sat down to start typing, he decided to go ahead and do the dishes.

Chapter 85

After putting the dishes away, Jeremy took a survey of his apartment to see if there were any other jobs that might pop up just when he was starting to get into the swing of his writing. He inventoried the rooms, examined every item made of plaster or fabric, and finally discovered that the curtains were a bit dirty. He removed all of the curtains from his windows and carried them to the one-hour dry cleaner's. He spent the next hour waxing the hardwood floors of his apartment. After he got back from the dry cleaner's with the curtains, he spent an hour putting them back onto their rods and hanging them on the windows. He then stood back and gazed around at the cleanliness of his apartment. By his reckoning he would not have another distraction for at least six months, which was how long he assumed that the first draft of *Fireface* would take to write. Of course, this did not include doing the dishes each night. He gave some thought to making a list of all of the potential distractions that might come along to interrupt his writing so that he would know ahead of time and be prepared for them. But then he decided to go ahead and take a chance and just start writing his novel. If distractions were going to come, they were going to come, and there was very little he could do to halt their inevitable progress. He sat down at his typewriter, rolled a blank sheet of paper through the platen, and typed: "They were so powerful that the flames that shot out of his face could melt army tanks."

The~~[garbled typewriter text]~~

Chapter 86

After typing this sentence, Jeremy leaned back in his chair and squinted at the words. He wanted to make certain that they were exactly right because he did not want to have to revise the entire novel after he got to the end. His plan was to make each sentence perfect so that not only would revision be rendered irrelevant, but he might even be able to send out the original typescript. After a minute he got up and went to the kitchen and brewed a fresh pot of coffee. He poured himself a full cup, strolled back into the living room, sat down at his typewriter, and stared at the sentence again. He began mouthing the words "melt . . . army . . . tanks." He rather liked this phrase. It had the quality of foreshadowing. It would be nice if he could get some symbolism into his novel too. Foreshadowing and symbolism. With those two classic literary techniques buttressing his novel, publication would damn near be a lock. All the New York editors would see that he was in the know when it came to writing prose fiction. He sipped at his coffee and stared at the sentence, and after a while he whispered, "Army," and started thinking about his army days. He recalled his first day in the foxhole. It had seemed like the general was never going to stop yelling at him. He finally shook himself out and typed another sentence. "The man was known throughout the land as Fireface, and people feared him." Jeremy softly muttered, "People . . . feared . . . him." This struck a familiar chord in his memory. Wasn't this what they called "telling rather than showing"?

Chapter 87

A gnawing sense of uneasiness began to envelop Jeremy. It occurred to him that he was probably going to have to create scenes showing people being afraid of Fireface. God only knew how many pages, or even chapters, that would take. He suddenly wished he had a pipe. He remembered how his ability to think had increased on the night he first smoked a pipe. He rubbed his right jaw where the flames had turned the tips of the hairs of his beard into funny little balls. The beard seemed to be getting back to normal. But he decided it probably wasn't a good idea to go out and buy a pipe, especially since he lived alone. If he was ever going to become a successful novelist, he would just have to make it to the top without one. Naked to the elements, alone and unaided. Although he might buy a pipe to use for his portrait that would appear on the back of his novel's dust jacket. Then a new plot twist came to him. What if instead of Fireface's face shooting out fire, Fireface set fire to other people's faces? That would certainly make people fear him. Jeremy thought about this idea for a while, then asked himself why anyone would go around setting people's faces on fire. What precisely would be the underlying motive? Money? Would this be some sort of clever blackmail scheme on the part of Fireface? But after mulling this over for a while, he asked himself why a guy who could set people's faces on fire would need money. A guy like that could just take anything he wanted without paying for it.

Chapter 88

Jeremy's inability to come up with any logical reason for Fireface to even exist eventually caused him to drop the idea of writing a crass commercial novel. He decided it was probably best to just go ahead and stick with producing immortal art. None of the deathless novels he had ever read got bogged down with clever plots. He recalled the disdain that his creative-writing teacher in college had seemed to hold for the concept of plotting. If a student asked him how a writer should go about plotting a piece of fiction, whether a short story or a novel, the teacher would just stare at the student as if he had said something inappropriate, or even obscene. In a way, Jeremy was disappointed that he had given up on a novel that would have made him wealthy, while at the same time he did feel rather noble. He decided that it was his craving to possess lots of money that had caused him to turn his back on great art. No great artist had ever made any money, except Hemingway and Faulkner and Fitzgerald and a couple other guys, but they certainly were not the norm. Most great writers died penniless, and while Jeremy neither wanted to die nor be penniless, he felt that he just might be able to tread the fine line between crass commercialism and immortal art by writing realistic novels about regular people, with no monster stuff or exciting action scenes that might be labeled a "plot" by the New York literary critics. He worried a great deal about the label that the critics would one day bestow upon his body of work.

Chapter 89

Now that Jeremy had abandoned commercial fiction, he was faced with the problem of writing authentic stories drawn from his own life experiences, and he really didn't have all that many to draw upon. It's true that he had been in a war and had seen the face of death, but that theme had been done to death. Jeremy finally decided that the solution to the problem would be to go out into the world and try to have some "real-life" experiences that he could turn into art. One day he drove to the bank and withdrew all of the money he had saved up as a cab driver, which amounted to four thousand dollars. He went to a surplus store and browsed the aisles looking for equipment that would make him look like a highly experienced hitchhiker. He purchased a backpack and two hobnailed boots. From this time forward he would be a vagabond of the road, searching the highways and byways for the true meaning of America. That theme had been done to death too, but it was the only other theme he could think of. He went home and stuffed as many of his earthly belongings as he could into the backpack, except his typewriter, which he planned to carry so he could immediately capture his ideas in prose while he was roaming the byways. He stepped outside of his apartment, planted his feet on the sidewalk, and stood for a few moments smiling up at the sun. This was the beginning of a new life. He stepped out on the left foot and hiked all the way across the city to the bus station, where he bought a one-way ticket to Tucson.

Chapter 90

Jeremy fell asleep on the bus, so he didn't get to see any of the western landscape that he had been looking forward to turning into words in the same way that Ansel Adams had turned mountains into photos. But he didn't sleep very well on the bus, so he was worn out by the time he got to Tucson. He hiked out of the bus terminal and went to a Motel 6, rented a room, and slept for twelve hours, only to be awakened by one of the maids. He put on his backpack and left the motel and started looking around downtown Tucson, excited about being in the heart of the wild west, and hoping that he might see a lot of raw cowboys. He was a bit disappointed when he found that there did not seem to be any cowboys in Tucson, just a lot of regular people. From there he took a bus to Flagstaff and stayed in a Holiday Inn. He saw a guy wearing a cowboy hat in Flagstaff but he was a cashier in an Arby's. From there Jeremy took a bus to Needles and spent the night at a Quality Inn. From there he took busses to Reno, Portland, Yakima, and Butte. By the time he got back home he was penniless. Someone had snuck into his motel room in Butte and stolen his backpack, where he kept his extra money in a secret canvas pocket. When he got to his apartment he slept for two days. After he woke up he walked all the way to The Cork Room. He couldn't wait to tell his friends about his adventures. He strode into the bar, grinned at the writers, and said loudly, "Gentlemen, my search for America has ended!"

Chapter 91

Jeremy waited expectantly to see baffled as well as intrigued expressions sprout on the faces of all of his friends, but the only response came from Hames, who hollered, "Hey Fireface, where've you been keeping yourself?" Controlling his facial expression, Jeremy walked over to the table and sat down with a heavy sigh, and told everyone that he had been on the road, traveling the highways and byways, scouring the sad heart of America in search of the truth. "I did that when I was eighteen," Hames said. Then Rod Lofton chimed in and said he had gone on the road too, and had gotten busted in Barstow on a frame-up involving stolen antiques and had pulled six months in a county jail. This had become the basis for the short story that had appeared in *Frogblade Magazine*. He reached into his tweed jacket and pulled out a well-thumbed copy of *Frogblade* and held it up in case anybody here had not read it yet. At this point the conversation turned into a kind of gleeful shouting match as all of the writers told wild stories about their lives on the open highway that none of them had been able to turn into successful novels. Some of the writers had traveled to foreign countries, such as Mexico and Canada, where they had gotten into terrible fixes with the locals. The stories became more outrageous, with each writer trying to top the last one. The men grew so noisy and laughed so hard at the incredible adventures that none of them noticed when Jeremy slipped out the door, leaving a shot of red wine on the table.

Chapter 92

One May afternoon Jeremy Bannister sat in his cab at the airport and started adding up the years. Come this June he would be twenty-five years old. That seemed an incredibly old age for a person to be. Where did all the time go? He thought back to his grade-school days when he used to sit by himself on the playground and pretend to be a big-shot novelist while all the other kids played kickball and laughed and pointed at him. Most of those kids were now stuck in boring careers and earning a lot of money. But he sincerely doubted that any of them were happy, even the kids who were married and had kids and owned big houses. He did not understand how anybody could possibly be happy doing anything except pursuing a successful career in the arts. He knew that as soon as he got published he would be happy forever. But according to his original plan, he ought to have become a big-shot novelist five years ago. And not only that, he had fully expected to be living in a big mansion by the age of twenty-five, and would be a retired millionaire who would write only if the urge to express himself overwhelmed him. What had happened? Why hadn't any of those dreams come true yet? Then a horrible thought occurred to him. What if the next twenty-five years were just like the last? What if he ended up being a fifty-year-old man who was still unpublished? He gazed blankly out the windshield for a while, then shook it out. That was a ridiculous notion. How could anybody possibly be fifty years old and still unpublished?

Chapter 93

When June arrived and Jeremy turned twenty-five, he began to get the odd feeling that there was something missing from his life besides acceptance slips. It was something more nebulous. He felt a dissatisfaction that came from a source that he was not able to identify. When he got up each morning he sometimes wondered why he was even bothering to go to work. The only thing he was getting out of it was money. Yet he knew he couldn't live without food and a place to rent, which was the only thing he got out of money. He had once assumed that he would be happy having only a little bit of money, but he had lately started thinking that only having a lot of money would make him happy. Then one day he was sitting in the cab line outside a hotel when he saw a businessman and a woman enter the lobby, and he suddenly realized that he was lonely. From the day that he had left home to make his way in the world he had been concentrating so hard on becoming a big-shot novelist that he had never given romance much thought, except in terms of subplots. Already one-third of his life had gone by, and he had never even been laid. How could he ever hope to compete with guys like Norman Mailer with a track record like that? Jeremy had always assumed that he would first publish a million-dollar bestseller, and then he would marry a beautiful buxom blonde bombshell. That was his basic plan. He had viewed this procedure as really no different from putting a car into gear and popping the clutch.

Chapter 94

The following weekend Jeremy decided that rather than go to The Cork Room and hang out with all the losers, he would go to a new discotheque that had recently opened. According to a conversation he had overheard between two cabbies at the airport, this place was supposed to be the swingingest joint in town. It was called The Martini Room. On Saturday afternoon Jeremy took a bus to the mall to pick out a suit suitable for dancing at a disco. The last suit he'd ever worn was an army uniform, so he wasn't up on the latest styles. He went to Wards and Sears and JCPenney and looked over the merchandise. He wanted to go into a store that specialized in men's clothing, but he hated the way salesmen were drawn to him like wolves to a downed cow. He bought a suit at JCPenney, and a new pair of shoes. He was hoping to impress as many women as he could. When he was younger his plan had been to impress women with his millions so it wouldn't matter what he looked like, but if he waited for that to happen he would probably never get laid. He took the bus back home and put on his new clothes and stood in front of the bathroom mirror and examined himself with a critical eye. He thought he looked pretty sharp. Since he was alone in the bathroom, he winked at himself in the mirror. He felt that for the first time in his life he was going to be making his intentions blatantly obvious. One look at this snazzy getup and every woman in The Martini Room would know exactly what he was up to.

Chapter 95

That night Jeremy went to the bus stop and waited for the Number 11. After he climbed onto the bus he decided to stand near the rear, since most of the seats seemed to have either sticky juice or hobos on them. Even though his new suit made him feel confident, he began to feel a little bit out of his element after he stepped off the bus outside The Martini Room and walked up to the door where a line of customers had formed. There was a black man standing outside the door acting as a kind of bouncer and deciding who got into the club and who didn't. He stared at Jeremy for a bit, then said, "Did you just get off that fucking bus?" The other customers began turning to stare at Jeremy. Some of them began quietly snickering. Half of the people were beautiful women, and the rest were their dates. Jeremy suddenly felt that no matter what he said, it would be the wrong answer, so he decided to just tell the truth and go back home. "Yes," he said, swallowing hard. He had known enough black dudes in the army to know that he had just done something that wasn't cool. But then the bouncer grinned and said, "Oh man, you so square you hip," and told him to step on inside. Jeremy went inside ahead of all the other customers, feeling kind of special. Nobody had ever called him "hip" before. It was noisy in the club, and except for the flashing strobes it was hard to see where he was walking. He kept bumping into people dancing to the music. The place was so packed that it took him ten minutes to figure out where the bar was.

Chapter 96

Jeremy had gotten good at calculating the difference between wine and beer, but he had never drunk any alcohol in the genre of "hard stuff." He could not have described the difference between bourbon and tequila if he was being interrogated by communist soldiers. In spite of this, he was eager to learn the differences because he felt that the night might come when he would find himself treating a beautiful woman to a drink, and he didn't want to make a complete fool out of himself by not being in the know. Even though he hated jobs per se, he was always interested in learning a new skill, or finding out the most effective way to avoid making bad mistakes. That night he found out that The Martini Room was so called because the only drinks it sold across the bar were martinis. That was the club's gimmick. So Jeremy's introduction to hard stuff consisted solely of gin and vermouth. Utilizing his knowledge of wines, he decided that one martini was probably equal to four glasses of pink Chablis. He ordered a drink and stood watching the people dance, bobbing his head to the beat of the music and trying to fit in. He had practiced doing this in his apartment while listening to the disco-music station, but he did not really know how to dance to disco music. He was a bit intimidated by the athletic nature of the moves. He was sipping what he figured was his eighth glass of pink Chablis and was still sober when a beautiful woman sidled up to him and shouted over the disco music, "What's your sign?"

Chapter 97

Jeremy immediately felt inadequate. He didn't have the slightest idea what she meant by that. In order to cover up his ignorance though, he manipulated his facial expression into that of delighted amusement, and nodded quickly. The woman frowned at Jeremy, and shouted, "I said what's your sign!" Jeremy's heart sank. He realized that there were certain customs and traditions in the disco world that he would have to both learn and master if he was ever going to get laid. He suddenly had the urge to rush out of the dancehall as if he had a pressing engagement, or maybe he could touch his fingers to his ears and pretend to be deaf. But this woman had probably seen him bobbing his head and would know he was faking it. He knew that by acting hip he had bitten off more than he could chew. Trapped and unable to think of a way out of this mess, he swallowed the contents of his martini glass and set it down. There was only one thing to do. He would have to try honesty again. "I don't know!" he yelled. The woman grinned at him and nodded. She was beautiful. Her hair was short and black and sort of frizzy, and she was wearing a slinky dress. "You're a Virgo!" she shouted. "I can always tell about things like that!" Jeremy was truly impressed. He wondered if it was the way he walked. He wasn't quite certain, but the woman seemed to be giving him "the eye." He asked if he could treat her to a fresh martini, and she nodded. When the drinks came, Jeremy handed her a glass. "You sure have big tits," he almost said.

Chapter 98

It began to occur to Jeremy that this Saturday night in the swingingest joint in town just might mark the beginning of his first true romantic relationship and the end of his zodiac sign. He and the woman went out to the main floor and began disco dancing, which Jeremy managed to pull off effectively because he'd been watching everybody else do it. Whenever they raised their arms or began batting their elbows, he did the exact same thing. It was almost like being in the army, and was as exhausting as push-ups. During the second record the woman told him that her name was Shantay. Jeremy didn't ask her last name. He thought it would be anticlimactic. By now he calculated that he already had imbibed the equivalent of twenty-four glasses of red wine and was surprised at how well he was holding his liquor. After the third record ended, Shantay asked him if he had a car, and he said "Yes, a taxi." Shantay asked him if he would be interested in taking her home, and he said, "Okay." It was only after they had left the club and were standing at the bus stop that Shantay apparently realized what he had meant. "You drive a taxi?" she said. Jeremy nodded and said, "But it's not here right now. I only drive it when I'm driving." Shantay squinted at him and said, "So how are we gonna get to your place?" Thinking quickly, Jeremy hurried back into the club. He picked through his bus money and called Yellow Cab. After he hung up he hurried outside and was surprised to find Shantay still standing there.

Chapter 99

After they got inside his apartment, Jeremy decided to ask Shantay a question that he had been wanting to ask ever since he'd met her. "Do you smoke?" He had been so concerned about making the acquaintance of a smoker in The Martini Room that he had gone out earlier that day and bought three different brands of cigarettes, one of them menthol and one non-filter, just in case the woman wanted to smoke afterwards, since a lot of women in novels smoked afterwards. But Shantay told him that she didn't smoke. She also said that she normally didn't go home with guys she had just met in bars. Jeremy didn't quite know how to interpret this statement, so he simply controlled his facial expression and tried not to think about it. He asked Shantay if she wanted a beer, and she said yes. Things seemed to be going smoothly. Jeremy went to the icebox and pulled out two beers and handed her one. She asked if he had a glass, and he said, "I'm sorry, but I don't own any glasses." He offered her a coffee cup, but she said no thanks. Jeremy then turned on his radio and searched the dial until he found the romantic-music station. They sat down on the couch and drank off their beers, then they began necking. A few minutes later she asked him where the bedroom was. Afterwards she told him that her last name was Halmerton and she worked as a receptionist in an insurance office in a suburban business park. Jeremy said he had dropped off businessmen there in his cab. He thought this was a rather romantic coincidence.

Chapter 100

As soon as Shantay woke up the next morning she told Jeremy to phone for a cab. Jeremy offered to fix her a plate of scrambled eggs, since James Bond often did this in his novels on the morning after. But she said that the thought of food made her want to vomit. There were a few minutes of awkward silence as they waited for the taxi to arrive. Jeremy wanted to ask her if they could go out again, but some instinct that he had long ago learned to listen to told him to remain silent. After Shantay left without saying goodbye, Jeremy dashed to his typewriter and tried to put down his feelings about his unique experiences of the night before. He had read a great many mainstream novels that had sex scenes in them, and he was satisfied with the verisimilitude that the authors had employed. Previously he had been concerned that if he ever got around to writing a sex scene in a novel, it might not come off as authentic. His creative-writing teacher in college had said, "Write what you know about" and now that Jeremy had overcome this literary obstacle he felt confident about writing any kind of novel at all that required a sex scene. He sat at his desk trying to recall with accuracy the series of events that had led up to the denouement of his brief tryst. He wanted to give it as much verisimilitude as possible. The crucial event itself hadn't lasted quite as long as most of the sex scenes did in Norman Mailer's novels, but at least Shantay hadn't started growling, "Do you love me?" like Dolores used to do.

Chapter 101

As Jeremy wrote about his first carnal encounter, the memory of it began to seem even more real than the actual event itself. He couldn't stop thinking about it. Even when he was driving his cab on Monday, the night kept running through his mind. Not all of it, but certain parts, like the parts of an R-rated movie that they don't show you in the previews. Jeremy began envisioning what his life would be like if he and Shantay went steady. There would be lots of dates, dancing, and possibly even scrambled eggs. Later that afternoon he drove to the business park and found the office where Shantay worked. He wanted to ask her for another date. When Jeremy walked into the office, Shantay looked up seemingly surprised to see him. "Would you like to go out on another date with me next Saturday?" he said. Shantay glanced around the office as if worried that someone might be listening to their conversation. The office was filled with men seated in cubicles and talking briskly on telephones. "What about the beard?" she whispered. "What about it?" Jeremy said. "It has to go," Shantay said. "Why?" Jeremy said. "Because I don't like it," she said. When Jeremy got back home that evening he shaved off his beard, then gave Shantay a quick phone call to let her know that the job was done and the date was on. He had not really wanted to shave, but he forced himself to do it because Shantay had told him that otherwise she wouldn't give him her phone number—and also because he wanted to have sex again.

Chapter 102

The following Saturday night Jeremy met Shantay at The Martini Room, where they danced to disco music until Shantay said she was ready to leave. Jeremy had wanted to pick her up at her apartment in a hired taxi, but she had told him that she didn't want him to know where she lived. Jeremy had assumed that she was being coy, and this made her all the more attractive. After their second date came to its climactic ending, Shantay told Jeremy that she was not about to date a man who smoked cigarettes, and that he would have to give them up. When Jeremy told her that he did not smoke, Shantay told him that she had found three full packs of cigarettes in his chest of drawers. "Don't lie to me," she said. "I will not date a liar." Feeling like an escaped convict trapped by a searchlight, Jeremy swallowed hard and told her that he would quit. Even if he was an aspiring writer who believed in always telling The Truth, he did not want to jeopardize the possibility of getting laid again. As the pair lay in bed staring at the ceiling, Shantay suddenly said, "What's all this about being a novelist?" Jeremy looked over at her and said, "Ever since I was a little kid I wanted to become a big . . . an author someday, and earn money writing best-selling novels." Shantay got up on one elbow and peered at him. "So what's the deal with cab driving?" Jeremy smiled and said, "That's what I do now to get money." Shantay shook her head no. "The cab driving and the writing have got to go. You're going to get a real job, buster." Then she kissed him.

Chapter 103

It was strange, Jeremy was to reflect later on. Even though Shantay had never actually said that she loved him, or asked him if he loved her, and even though he didn't ask her to marry him, Shantay began talking about wedding plans. She had brought up the subject at some point that he could not exactly pinpoint. She would talk about it whenever they were lying in bed or on the couch or on the throw rug that she had made him buy. She calculated how many invitations they would have to send out, and who her maids of honor would be, and how much a caterer would cost. Jeremy would lie next to her, frowning like a guy trying to get a word in edgewise, except he never said a word. He would listen to Shantay going on about her plans, hoping that at some point she would laugh and say she was just kidding. And when she wasn't talking about her wedding plans, she was reminding Jeremy that it was time for him to either go to an employment agency or start scanning the want ads. Jeremy felt the same way he had felt when he had received his draft notice. He felt the same way he had felt when his landlady had asked him to rake the leaves, the way he had felt when he had lived in a seedy hotel in college. He felt he was not entirely in control of his life. Whenever he thought about bringing up the fact that he had never proposed to her, Shantay would have sex with him, and this would cause him to stop thinking about all the things he was thinking about. It was as if Shantay could read his mind.

103

Chapter 104

One Saturday night while Jeremy was trying to write a novel, the phone rang. He refused to pick it up. He knew it was Shantay. She would want to discuss her wedding plans in vivid detail. Any day now she was certain to tell him the precise date that he would be giving up his bachelorhood. Whenever she asked him if he had looked for a job, he lied and said yes. Then she would ask him where he had applied for work, and he would give her the names of companies that he had culled from the want ads. He felt like a scoundrel who was cheating on his unemployment benefits. He listened to the phone ring until he couldn't stand it anymore. He put on his coat and fled his apartment, and walked the streets trying to think, but found it impossible. He finally decided to take a bus over to The Cork Room. When he walked into the bar he was hailed by all of the novelists whom he had not seen since . . . since . . . Jeremy could not recall the last time he had been in here, or anywhere else. After he had started dating Shantay, he no longer seemed to have a night life of his own. He was either with Shantay or was waiting for her to show up. He sat down at a table with his friends and ordered a shot of red wine, then tried to maintain control over his facial expression by fashioning a hearty smile that he hoped would cover up his true feelings. "Good lord, what's the matter with you?" Hames said, frowning with deep concern. "I'm not really all that certain," Jeremy said, "but I think I'm getting married."

Chapter 105

After the laughter had died down, the writers looked at Jeremy with fresh concern. It turned out that it was a custom for a cab writer in The Cork Room to feign horror whenever he announced that he was getting married. Thus, the writers at the table had assumed that Jeremy was merely taking part in this tradition by acting as if his life was falling down around his ears. There were many such traditions among the writers in The Cork Room, such as sending queries to literary agents, or applying for government grants, or entering writing contests and then grousing about their failure to win a prize, not to mention their railing against the unfairness of New York's publishers' row. But the panicked look in Jeremy's eyes and the trembling of his hands indicated that they had misinterpreted his facial muscles. It appeared from all indications that he was telling the truth. "You say you're not certain?" Hames said. Jeremy shook his head no, held his hands palm upward, and tried to explain the situation, but the only sound that came from his mouth was an odd "ack . . . ack . . . ack." Hames quickly asked a waitress for three shots of pink Chablis, then administered them to Jeremy like a medic. After downing the shots, Jeremy found his voice and began relating the vivid details of his relationship with Shantay, from the night they had first met in The Martini Room until the phone had started ringing forty-five minutes earlier. His friends listened with rapt attention, and tried to keep from laughing at regular intervals.

The...

Chapter 106

After Jeremy finished wringing the last detail out of his tragic story, Hames sat back and lit his pipe and took a few puffs, then pointed the stem at him. "You are living proof that a woman will marry anything," he said. There were mutters of general assent around the table. Jeremy frowned, not sure if he ought to take this as an insult. "The truth is," Hames said, "there are women in this world who do not marry for love. This might explain why she has never told you that she loves you. It is because she does not love you. If you look at the situation from her point of view, love and marriage are two separate concepts. They bear no relationship to each other. In a woman's world these concepts appear primarily in the lyrics of pop music, poetry, and commercial bodice rippers. But the actual reason she wants to marry you is because you are a man." This sounded like a compliment, but Jeremy wasn't certain. "In her eyes, you are fundamentally a tabula rasa, a blank slate, a formless and shapeless entity waiting for a woman to come along and put the finishing touches on the raw material of your being." Jeremy stared at him with uncomprehending eyes. Hames had lost him back at "tabula rasa." Jeremy had taken Latin during high school but had dropped out after the first quarter to take a course in auto-body repair, which he had failed. But the rest of the writers around the table began nodding as though Hames was vividly describing something that they were familiar with. Perhaps their own lives.

Chapter 107

"I'm sorry," Jeremy said desperately, "but I just don't understand what you're getting at." Hames smiled the weary, knowing smile of a man who has been through at least one divorce. "I'm simply saying that Shantay does not want to marry you so much as she wants to be married. After your honeymoon is over, she will immediately begin revising you to suit her vision of the ideal husband. I have noticed that you do not smoke, which as a writer does not speak well in your favor, but you are fortunate in that this is one aspect of your personality that she will not demand that you change." Jeremy perked up a bit. "It's funny that you should say that, because she once ordered me to give up smoking." Hames nodded wisely, and said, "Force of habit. The new Jeremy Bannister will be modeled loosely upon personality traits that she finds the most endearing, very likely those of her father. To her you are little more than an old tenement building waiting to be remodeled. This is probably the last time any of us will ever see you inside this bar. And should one of us happen to pass you on the street in the future, he doubtless will not recognize you. When you walked into The Cork Room earlier, I had trouble recognizing you without your beard. Consider that the tip of an ominous iceberg, my friend." As he took all this in, Jeremy started to feel faint, and even a bit frightened. "But what am I going to do?" he groaned. The writers glanced at each other, but no one offered a solution. They were collectively stumped.

Chapter 108

Jeremy did not receive any more phone calls after that night, but then, on the following Tuesday, he received an envelope filled with want ads clipped from the newspapers by Shantay, who added a note telling him, "There's no time like the present to start thinking about a career." Jeremy began to feel like a character in a movie being stalked by an insane woman who otherwise looked normal. If there was a sudden knock on his door, his stomach began to tie itself in knots. He had trouble eating, and he began to both leave and enter his apartment by the bathroom window. When he drove his cab he pondered the predicament that he had somehow gotten himself into. He wanted badly to continue with his writing career, as well as to make The Big Money at it, and the one thing that Jeremy had learned from his checkered employment history was that, while there were a lot of jobs worse than cab driving, there were none better. Thus, he would not be able to continue his writing career, not even in secret, throughout his marriage to Shantay, for no matter what job he might obtain in the future, it would drain him of all strength. The notion of becoming a secret novelist while he was married was an option that he had seriously considered. He might be able to write in the bathroom while his wife was asleep. These fancy new electric typewriters on the market were said to be as silent as a whisper. Even though Jeremy had never sat down to plan what to do with his life, he decided that the time had come to plan what not to do.

Chapter 109

Jeremy sat on his couch throughout the entire night, and tried to think. Around 3 a.m. it occurred to him to call his old roommate Fontaine and ask him what to do. In spite of his intense dislike for him, the guy always seemed to have an answer for everything. But he decided that calling Fontaine so late would be rude. The next morning he made the boldest move of his entire literary career. He didn't shave again. He went to work feeling like a new man, having revived the beard that he had worn before he had ever gotten laid. It would be his flag of independence. The way he figured it, if he stayed away from The Martini Room for the rest of his life, and changed his phone number, he would never see Shantay again. That night she showed up at his door and said, "I see you forgot to shave this morning, honey. What do you say we go into the bathroom and I'll watch you shave? I expect to be doing that every morning for the rest of my life." Jeremy backed away from her and looked around his apartment frantically. He snatched up his typewriter and held it tightly to his chest. Shantay frowned at it, then put her fists on her hips and started tapping her right toe. "I thought I told you to get rid of that thing." Jeremy didn't recall her having said any such thing, although she might have said it in a symbolic manner. He began breathing rapidly and making that peculiar ack-ack-ack sound. "What in the hell is wrong with you?" Shantay said. Jeremy took a deep breath and let it out slowly. "I'm already married," he lied.

Chapter 110

In his entire literary career Jeremy had never been so creative. The words that spilled forth from his mouth were like spontaneous prose. It would later remind him of the times in college when he had written term papers just minutes before they were due. It was as though his thoughts were being transcribed to paper by a speed typist. He told Shantay that he had a wife and three children in Tucson, and that he had recently visited them to see how they were doing, and they were doing just fine. For the first time since Shantay had met him, she seemed at a loss for words. She then asked why Jeremy wasn't living with his family. He replied that he and his wife had been having serious marital problems, and his wife had told him to take some time off to decide whether it was going to be her or his writing ambitions. Shantay's jaw dropped. She took her fists off her hips and pointed at him. "Why in the hell didn't you tell me you were a married man?" she snarled. Jeremy shrugged. "Because I'm still trying to decide whether it's going to be her." Shantay began staring at him with her head cocked at a suspicious angle. Then she gave him the fish-eye. "If you're married, how come I don't see the indent of a wedding ring on your third finger?" Jeremy thought fast. "Because we're hippies," he said. Shantay shook her head with disgust, called him a dirty bastard, and stormed out the door. The next morning Jeremy woke up on the floor where he had fainted dead away, still clutching his typewriter.

Chapter 111

The only thing that bothered Jeremy about telling all those incredible lies was that one day he might write a bestseller and Shantay might learn that he wasn't married and would come after him. He had never seen any woman quite as angry as Shantay had been. But he realized that, given the state of his writing career, probably the least of his worries was being stalked by a woman scorned. He then wondered if it would be possible to write a novel about an angry bitch stalking a poor sap. He knew at least as much about that aspect of life as he knew about sex. But that particular theme had been done to death by screenwriters. In fact, it seemed like every idea he had ever managed to come up with had been picked over by other writers, even writers whom he wouldn't have considered his equal if he was a published writer. Things had gotten so bad that whenever he thought up an idea for a book, he would check the bestseller lists to see if someone had already beaten him to it. Jeremy was outraged at the ridiculous ideas that some writers had managed to sell for millions of dollars. He felt certain that he could think up ridiculous ideas. Yet even when he came up with regular ideas for stories, he couldn't come up with any decent endings. And it seemed like the worst writers made the most money. James Joyce hadn't made any money off his books, so how could writers who wrote worse than James Joyce get rich? There were mysterious factors at play within the publishing industry that were beyond Jeremy's ken.

Chapter 112

After his near miss with Shantay, Jeremy decided to buckle down and start planning his life a little better. It had been out of control long enough. But since the only thing he wanted to do was write, he knew that he would have to start planning his novels better too. This thought depressed him because he did not know how to plan a novel. His creative-writing teacher in college had told the class that planning novels ahead of time would destroy their creativity and turn their books into plastic. But given the success of Jeremy's last desperate plan, it seemed like a viable approach. If he did write a plastic novel, he could always use a pseudonym so that none of the students in his class would know that he had disobeyed their teacher. He thought about taking a shot at trying to write *Fireface* again, but he was still unable to figure out why anyone would act the way Fireface was supposed to act. On top of that, he lived with a constant fear that a novel titled *Fireface* would appear in a bookstore, or else a horror film called *Fireface* would suddenly appear in the theaters. Jeremy would plan each book as best he could, trying to think up some kind of a conflict, and as much foreshadowing as he could muster, but he always put off thinking up an ending in the hopes that the climax would just come to him when he got close to the last page. The seasons came and went. By the time Jeremy turned thirty years old, he had written ten unfinished novels and did not have a single rejection slip to show for them.

Chapter 113

Jeremy had stopped going to The Cork Room years ago. It had given him an eerie feeling to be sitting among writers who never seemed to get published, or to see newer and younger unpublished writers who drifted into the bar and became a part of the scene like dead sea creatures forming part of a coral reef. One evening a young man had come into the bar who had once published a suspense thriller in paperback. After getting over their initial shock, all the writers began questioning him intensely about how to get an agent, but he said he didn't know how to get one and had handled his own book contract. After that the writers began ignoring him, and he soon drifted away. At the age of thirty Jeremy felt the way he expected to feel at fifty, if he was still unpublished at fifty. He began to suspect that he was going to be driving a cab all his life, which he didn't really mind, except it was a job, and his dream had always been not to have a job. If he didn't have a job, then he would have the time and energy to write a novel that would be good enough to make him so rich that he wouldn't have to have a job. The only thing he ever felt like doing anymore was watching TV. He couldn't recall when he had bought his TV. It was sometime in his late twenties, but he couldn't pinpoint the exact year. "Frickit all," Jeremy growled to himself one evening as he sat watching *Rat Patrol*. "If I ever get rich off a novel, I'll never write another word again as long as I live." Jeremy Bannister had made his last artistic statement.

113

Chapter 114

"Good Christ, is that you, Bannister?" said a familiar voice from the rear of Jeremy's cab as he pulled away from the airport terminal. He glanced around and saw that the businessman who had hopped into the back was Fontaine. He looked exactly the same as he had back in college, except that he was wearing a snazzy three-piece suit. Jeremy quickly turned around and gazed out the windshield, but he could see Fontaine squinting at him in the rearview mirror. Jeremy tried hard to control his facial expression, but he had lost the ability to do that on the day he had turned thirty. Instead he thought about simply lying, but he had never been able to pull that off around Fontaine. "Yes, my name is Bannister," he said quickly, pretending he didn't know his old roommate and hoping the guy wouldn't ask pointed questions. Fontaine smirked. "So you're still driving a goddamn taxi, huh?" Jeremy gave up all pretense at pretense, and nodded. Fontaine leaned over the back of Jeremy's seat. Jeremy felt as if he was seated in the presence of a hanging judge. "What's with the spaghetti strainer?" Fontaine said. Jeremy glanced at him and shrugged. "I got tired of paying for shaving cream." Fontaine smirked and said, "Are you still trying to be a big-shot novelist?" Jeremy sighed. It had been a long time since he had used that phrase in mixed company. "No, I guess I've sort of lowered my sights on that deal," he said. "I'm just trying to be a regular novelist." Fontaine nodded and said, "There's hope for you yet, Bannister."

Chapter 115

Jeremy didn't feel especially comfortable sitting there discussing his life's ambitions with Fontaine, just as it had made him feel like holing up in his room back in the shanty that he and Fontaine had shared in college. But he was stuck with driving Fontaine to the city, so he did what he often did when he had an undesirable fare in the rear of his taxi: he drove a little faster. He peered into the rearview mirror and said, "So what are you doing with your life?" Fontaine grinned big. "I'm a certified public accountant. I handle all of the financial matters for Magnitude Unlimited." MU was the biggest company in the entire world. "That must be boring work," Jeremy said with a smirk. "You bet it is," Fontaine said, "but the pay is unbelievable." Jeremy remained quiet for the rest of the trip. After they got downtown, Fontaine asked to be dropped off at the Hilton, then handed Jeremy a fifty and said, "Keep it." Jeremy took it and kept it. "Listen here, Bannister, it's obvious that you didn't take my advice. If you had, you and I would be doing lunch today. So I'm going to say this one more time. Forget James Joyce. Crank out some commercial garbage. That's where the real money is. I ought to know. MU owns half the publishing companies in America." For one moment Jeremy thought he might be able to get an "in" from Fontaine, but the idea of asking a big favor from his former roommate revolted him. "If you ever write anything commercial, let me know," Fontaine said. "I can give you an 'in' with a publisher."

Chapter 116

Jeremy watched Fontaine enter the Hilton, then he sat pondering Fontaine's offer. The prospect of having an "in" with a publisher thrilled the aspiring writer in him, but the rest of him knew that having an "in" did not really amount to much if he didn't have a novel ready to be submitted, and according to the piles of unfinished manuscripts lying around his apartment, he didn't. He drove the rest of the day feeling like a wino peering through the window of a locked liquor store. That evening as he sat drinking beer and staring at his television, he considered the irony of the fact that he now had a publisher, so to speak, but he didn't have a finished manuscript ready to be submitted to an editor. This seemed like the exact opposite of the way reality was supposed to work. He wondered if he might be able to think up an ending for one of his manuscripts and finish it, but he had spent the last five years trying to think up endings for ten books and hadn't had any luck. He didn't know how to get any of the characters out of the terrible fixes they were in. Some of the books were genre, and some were great art. He had expected the art books to be the easiest to end, but he had been wrong. He changed the channels with his remote-control device and watched a few minutes of *Starsky & Hutch*. Then he switched to *Bewitched*. What had happened to all of his artistic values? On the TV, two empty shoes were strolling across Samantha's floor. "That's the kind of garbage the masses want," he snarled. "Magic shoes."

Chapter 117

After *Bewitched* was over, Jeremy sat thinking about magic shoes. Suppose he wrote a book about a man who has a pair of evil boots. Maybe the man finds the boots in his closet and doesn't know where they came from, so he puts them on and they immediately walk him to a cemetery and launch him into an open grave. Think how horrible that would be. But how would the book end? Maybe some shoeshine boy in the know would save the day with a can of magic Kiwi polish that thwarts evil. Jeremy idly began wondering if it was the TV or the beer that was rotting his brain. Then he started thinking that he might be able to write the evil-boot novel using a flamboyant style like that of James Joyce, incorporating archaic words that would not only obscure the plot, but render it irrelevant. He decided it was the beer. It had already given him a potbelly. He was in terrible physical condition. The only exercise he got these days was putting luggage into taxi trunks. He had joined a gym a couple of years back with the idea of getting into shape. It had cost him three hundred dollars for a membership, but he had gone there only once. He had felt embarrassed trying to heft dumbbells among all the gigantic guys who looked like the Hulk. He recalled the kid who had lived across the street from him when he was a boy. The kid's dad had given him a set of barbells on his birthday. That bastard was getting rich nowadays winning national bodybuilding contests. Jeremy felt depressed. He wished he had a set of magic barbells.

Chapter 118

By the time Jeremy went to bed that night, he had come up with an idea for a horror-suspense genre novel about evil barbells. He decided not to drive his cab the next day. He wanted to stay home and think about this story idea. It was the only one he'd gotten excited about since dropping *Fireface*. The following morning he sat in his living room drinking beer and pondering all of the monster movies he had ever seen, and how they started, and how they ended, and all the stuff that went on in between. Suppose there's this kid who's always getting roughed up at school. One day he goes to a flea market and ends up buying a set of barbells from a weird old man who grins and cackles knowingly. The kid goes home and begins lifting weights, and immediately becomes gigantic. But his strength lasts only one day. Then his muscles shrink back to normal. At first the kid is frightened, but then he tries it again, and realizes he possesses a means of exacting vengeance against his multitude of enemies. He begins to view his set of barbells as some sort of supernatural friend. Later on in the story, bullies from the football team are found mysteriously beaten up. Rumors start to spread about a muscle-bound monster who has it in for loudmouth jocks. The whole town is in a tizzy. The cops are baffled. Jeremy got up from his chair and hurried to his typewriter. He rolled a blank sheet of paper through the platen and, without fidgeting or cracking his knuckles, he began typing a novel entitled *Barbells from Hell*.

Chapter 119

Desperate to follow through on an idea for once in his life, Jeremy spent two months working on his novel. Prior to this he had spent only a few weeks writing a novel before giving up on it. He had managed to get halfway through his earlier novels before he gave up because he had typed them as fast as possible, hoping to revise the novels at his leisure, including fixing the massive profusion of typos. On top of that, he had never outlined a novel completely from beginning to end. He had always put his faith in pure inspiration, making things up as he went along, which had never worked. But now he wrote slowly, and when he drove his taxi he carried a pocket notebook with him and jotted down ideas as they came to him. At night he would sit at his typewriter and flesh out the ideas. If he got stuck on a certain section, he would turn on his TV and watch a monster movie until he had recharged his creative batteries. At the end of two months, after the book was written, revised, and polished, Jeremy called the headquarters of Magnitude Unlimited and asked to speak with Mister Fontaine. "Good Christ, is that you, Bannister?" Jeremy explained that he had recently written a crass commercial novel that had no literary merit whatsoever, and asked if Fontaine might still be willing to give him an "in" with a publisher. "What's the book about?" Fontaine said, a wary note entering his voice. After Jeremy had described the plot and told him the title, Fontaine said, "You have got to be fucking kidding me."

Chapter 120

Barbells from Hell became the fastest-selling novel in the history of Magnitude Unlimited's subsidiary publishing company, Two-Fisted House. Even before the book hit the shelves, Jeremy began receiving calls from studio executives in Hollywood who wanted to buy the movie rights. Literary agents who had sent him rejection slips years ago began leaving messages on the answering machine that Jeremy had bought so that he wouldn't have to talk with them. One week after his novel hit the bookstores, it rose to the very top of every bestseller list in America. Even though Jeremy didn't want a literary agent, he found that he needed someone who could cut him favorable deals on the foreign editions, TV, audio, and DVD rights to the story. Jeremy quit his cab job and spent his time cruising around town in his new Cadillac, shopping for a big mansion. Three weeks after his novel hit the shelves, an autograph party was scheduled for him at the same bookstore where Damian Greenleaf Bordon had inscribed a novel for him. There was a massive crowd of people waiting in line to get their books signed, and the store owner was handing out numbers. None of the cab writers from The Cork Room had shown up, but standing at the very end of the line was Fontaine, his face devoid of anything resembling a smirk. After Jeremy signed Fontaine's book, he gave his old roommate a big smile, stood up from the table, and said, "Hey, let's go pop some corks," to a buxom blonde standing next to him.